OBSCURED
CONNECTIONS

JOHN W SMITH

WELL READ PRESS

BOOK AND COVER DESIGN BY NEMO DESIGNS

ALL RIGHTS RESERVED.

PUBLISHED IN THE UNITED STATES BY WELL READ PRESS

ORDERING INFORMATION:

SPECIAL DISCOUNTS ARE AVAILABLE ON QUANTITY PURCHASES BY CORPORATIONS, ASSOCIATIONS, AND OTHERS. FOR DETAILS CONTACT THE SPECIALS SALES DEPARTMENT AT JOHN W. SMITH, WELL RED PRESS, 12603 STATE ROUTE 143, SUITE G, #42, HIGHLAND, ILLINOIS 62249

(FICTION / FANTASY /DARK FANTASY / OCCULT / SUPERNATURAL

ISBN: 978-1-7325384-0-5

FIRST EDITION

PUBLISHER: WELL READ PRESS

12605 STATE ROUTE143, SUITE G #42

HIGHLAND, ILLINOIS 62249

JOHN W. SMITH

OTHER BOOKS
NIGHTMARES OF A MADMAN
DARK DREAMS
DEATH'S RETRIBUTION
TAINTED BLOOD
HEART OF A DRAGON
A DARK AND STORMY NIGHT, AN ANTHOLOGY
E-SHORT STORIES:

Colonial Scum
Hungry Things

For bulk orders contact writerphotographer1946@gmail.com

Author Website: www.johnwsmithauthor.com

�֍ Created with Vellum

CONTENTS

ACKNOWLEDGMENTS

This particular book of short stories has been years in the making. A few are older stories, never published, a couple published, now expanded, and placed here, plus new stories.

I thank all the people who encouraged me to do another book of short stories while writing much longer works. There are far too many friends and readers to mention, but they have my gratitude.

I also want to thank Sandy Maue for having the patience for editing this book. It has taken a while thanks to stay at home orders, and a multitude of personal and health problems with me.

Her mom, Barbara (Bitsy) Netemeyer, who did a final reading, out loud, which helped Sandy and me to find several small errors.

Special thanks to Shannon Nemechek for designing the cover, formatting, and uploading to KDP, Kindle and Draft2Digital.

Without her, I'm not sure who would do all that work. She is great in all areas and reasonably priced.

And Last but not least to all my readers. You keep me motivated and writing no matter how I feel physically. You make me very happy.

Thank you all

DEDICATION

This book is dedicated to Mr. Jaime "The Rebel" Cancio. Jim, as he was known by his friends, had every book I ever published and read just about every short story and other works I have written. We became friends in 1987 and discovered we celebrated the same birthday, month, day, and year. We became brothers until he died.

Jim was an interesting man, knowledgeable and willing to help anyone when asked. He would volunteer to help someone out of trouble if he saw a need, and the individual accepted.

He didn't always care for the type of stories I wrote, but he always had compliments about the story line, providing advice on ways to approach a variety of topics. He didn't just read, he would also make suggestions to improve the work. I agreed at times, argued at times, and ignored them at times. He never got mad and always asked when he could read the next work.

I miss this man and his suggestions to improve my work.

1

A SHORT COURTSHIP

THE COUPLE STROLLED through the garden on a warm spring day with the sun sparkling off the leaves of the plants. Hand in hand, they explored the maze of flora and fauna along the path. Some of the shrubs were trimmed shorter than the others and he could see over them and recognize the pattern of the maze.

Our third date, of sorts. I think it is time to move our relationship up a notch.

He enjoyed the scent of sage, thym-e, and rosemary, as well as the explosion of colors of the spring flowers.

"Last night's soft rain really turned the gardens into a thing of beauty and life." Lisa said, while leading him into catacombs and dead ends within the maze.

He didn't mind when Lisa periodically stopped to enjoy the beauty. It allowed him to do some admiring too. *She is beautiful, and she smells like a flower … lavender I do believe. She brings out thoughts of lust in me. He rubbed her arms and shoulder, his fingers slipping just an inch or two below the cowl of her dress. Perhaps I could love her someday.*

When they entered the Rose of Sharon warren situated near the end of the maze, he was amazed how the bushes had grown into ten-foot trees blocking the view ahead. Their time alone was about to end and his opportunity for making his intentions know was waning.

As they continued, he tilted his head as he heard the barking of the family hound. It had joined them last week, but today, it sounded like it was sitting on the porch.

The voices of three men filtered through the bushes. He recognized the deep voice of the young maiden's father as he gave assignments. The other two, presumably workmen, responded in kind.

He tightened his hold, on her arm as they continued their walk, until nearly reaching the end of the Rose of Sharon warren. Now was his chance. He stopped and turned her to him. Without warning, he gently kissed her and moaned as he was filled with the taste from her soft, sweet lips.

She stiffened, "You swine", she screamed, as she pushed him away. Stomping one foot with a huff, she pivoted and ran through the rest of the maze in tears.

Running to catch the girl, he tripped over an exposed root and fought the brambles and bushes. It was as though they were protecting her. At last, he saw the exit and witnessed the beauty falling into the arms of her father.

He stumbled, again, as he entered the courtyard. Falling face down in the dirt, he found himself stunned and out of breath.

Grabbing the handle of his pickaxe, her father marched over and stood beside him.

The suitor tried to roll over and stand up. If he could explain his actions. He knew the man's reputation of being protective with Lisa. If he could explain he was only trying to tell the man how he felt about the daughter, perhaps he could escape with his life.

The mountain of a man pinned him down with a foot between his shoulders.

"But sir." The suitor 's shout muffled. "I meant no harm."

"You disrespected my daughter." The father's voice dropped an octave yet remained calm and commanding. "I will not allow you to sully my daughter or another woman."

The old man tapped the suitor on his shoulders with the blade of the pickaxe. Using both hands, he raised it over his head and swung down hard. The blade connected with the back of the young man's neck. The sickening crunch of breaking bones ended the whining of the former suitor.

"This one showed promise." The old man said to Lisa as he looked over his shoulder. Smiling he pulled the blade of the pickaxe out of the boy's body. Blood flowed like water in a stream as he wrenched the point out of the neck, ripping the flesh.

"Lisa." The father ordered, "Get the wheelbarrow, and hall this … this thing out of the yard and feed it to the pigs."

Lisa tossed her former suitor's carcass into the barrow. She then rolled him to the far side of the barn. She stripped him, took his wallet, jewelry, and checked his teeth for gold fillings. Just before she dumped him over the short fence, she kissed his lips. "Almost my little piggy, almost. Another hundred yards would have made the difference between becoming a lover or lunch for the pigs."

She hummed a little tune as she returned to the house. *Well, that is six beasts failing a simple courtship. I hope number seven proves worthy of my love and accepts my proposal to the happy occasion of marriage.*

2

INNOCENT

THE PAIR RAN hell bent toward the entrance of the tunnel. They had no idea how long or how far they had run. Both had fallen several times. Now dried blood tracked down their shins and soaked into their socks and tennis shoes.

They stopped as the tunnel split into two directions. Looking down both openings, the boy saw a faint light at the end of the tunnel on the right and drug the girl with him.

"NO." She screamed, trying to pull away from the boy. "It's a trick, it will catch us again."

He gripped her hand tighter and dragged her down the tunnel. "Run!" he said, gasping for air.

They stumbled out of the mine at full speed. The sun was high in the sky providing needed warmth after their time in the caverns. They collapsed beside an abandoned rail car a little distance away from the mine entrance.

"It can't come out of the mine." He said. "If it could have escaped, everyone in town would have been acting like the kids in the cave before it devoured them." He paused, shaking his head. "With all their drinking, fighting, and ripping the clothes off each other, it grew strong enough for me to see it."

The girl's eyes were wide with fear, "It was some kind of

demon, feeding off all the energy the older kids were giving off. The thing sucked the life from them as they had wild sex. They were dropping dead as its strength grew."

Every few seconds he glanced at the mine entrance. "Do you remember how deep we were in the there? I was distracted by the loud music and sounds of the older teens."

She shook her head. "I was so afraid of the dark. The thoughts of rats and spiders had me in a panic. If you hadn't held my hand, I don't know what I would have done."

"I only found our way to the party because of all the noise. I was stimulated and followed the sounds. We entered the cavern and they paid no attention to us. It was arousing … at first. Then I saw it."

"I didn't see the thing until you started dragging me to the mouth of the cavern." She whispered. "It was growing and ugly. It stared at me with those glowing red eyes and I thought it was going to kill me next."

"I am glad we ran when we did. I was starting to feel like some kind of animal … urges I have never felt be for in such a primitive way …" he said, his voice quivered with fear. "I don't know how we found the right twists and turns to find the surface … but I am grateful."

The girl leaned into his shoulder. Her body both shivered and jerked from the power of her sobs.

He pulled her closer and she curled into his body like a second skin. He wrapped his other arm around her holding her tight with both arms until she wore herself out. Her sobs lost strength. She quit crying and shaking as she buried her face into his shoulder. Her body relaxed as his hands stroked her long blond hair and traveled down her back. She snuggled against him. Her lips touched his neck with what felt like a kiss. Her tongue snaked out and softly licked his skin.

He couldn't help himself. His hands dropped to her waist, massaging her, his hands climbed up her sides, reaching for private areas he knew he should ignore. He pushed her away,

"It's okay … we are safe, there is nothing to fear." He stammered as he felt those primal feelings growing in his body.

She leaned forward and kissed him on the lips. Her touch was more than he could handle. His desires overcame his control. He wanted her. It didn't matter that she was fourteen and he was fifteen. He knew what he had to have but didn't want to scare her, at least until he had her filled with desire.

"It's okay," he said, dropping one hand to the side of her hip, rubbing her thigh. "There is nothing to be afraid of. It's over now."

The urge to take her was almost out of control. Face red, with shame he realized he was prepared to rape her. *What has gotten into me?* He didn't understand what was happening, but he had to possess her.

She shoved him away.

When he no longer touched her, the urges disappeared. He stared into her beautiful, swirling eyes. "I'm sorry. I don't know what got into me or why I tried to touch you like that."

Her hands cupped his face. Eyes flashing red, and with a smile he had never seen on a girl, she said, "No, this is not how I want it. Not even close."

Her lips smashed into his. They were rough and strong. A thick, muscle filled, long, pointed, dove into his throat. She dropped her hands to his shoulders with talon like fingers and gripped him in a tight embrace. "Are you willing to give me your all … everything I desire?"

With her words, the passion hit him full force. He was ready to push her to the ground and mount her like a rutting deer.

Breaking the kiss, breathing deep, he stared into her flame filled eyes. "I want you more than anything" He howled.

"Give me your soul in exchange for my body." She laughed at his innocence. "My pleasures haven't started yet, but you are the beginning."

He lay paralyzed, as teeth lengthened into something akin to a giant shark. Her skin filled with large scales, and her fingernails grew to several inches with long sharp points. Grabbing his hair, she jerked his head back and to the side. Mouth wide, her face struck down, like a rattlesnake, biting deep into his throat.

His body jerked when her teeth pierced his skin. At first, he struggled. Her mind invaded his and he ceased fighting. As she took another deep mouth full of his blood and life force, he moaned.

In less than six helpings, he lay limp in her arms. She dropped him to the ground and watched the confusion on his face turn to horror. She tore part of his shirt and used it to wipe the crimson smile from her face.

She returned to her angelic human form. "You were right, Billy. The demon couldn't escape the mine on its own. But there were enough people partying that I, Balthazar, filled their heads with lust or hate and fed on their spirits and blood."

She looked at the mine entrance, her voice echoed and sounded like gravel being dumped on the street, "It gave me the strength to possess this pretty little thing. I kept you alive to help me find my way out of the darkness."

Balthazar turned toward the valley. The town spread over several square miles. She paused soaked in the humanity down below. "So many centuries have I sought release. Now I am free ... free to quench my hungers on the humans."

She took a deep breath and smelled the corruption of the people.

She mounted her bicycle. As she began to peddle, she looked back at the dead body. "You were wrong Billy, the town isn't about to be mangled ... the town's heart, soul and flesh is about to be devoured. And Billy dear, you showed me the way."

3

NEARLY DARK

THOMAS SPRANG UP, then instantly fell back onto the mattress. He pulled the covers up to his neck and hugged a pillow to his face as a scream buried itself among the feathers. With great effort, he slowed his breathing to normal and opened his eyes to fixate on a single spot on the ceiling.

The black thing with long, clawed arms and legs crept through his memory. Its giant maw stretched to reveal two rows of needle-sharp teeth. One chomp and it could swallow him whole.

The same dream, every night, for the last week, jolted him awake the moment the creature reached out to touch him.

Thomas shivered as a cold, unseen shroud of mist enveloped him. He had closed his windows and turned up the heat when he went to bed, yet there was no warmth. What he experienced now was how he felt in the dream when the creature appeared.

Was he actually awake, or caught in a dream within a dream?

He wiggled his toes, blinked several times, and forced his fingers to release the death grip on his pillow. Having completed this ritual, Thomas felt confident he was awake.

With a forceful nod, Thomas admonished himself. You coward. It was only a dream. *You're awake now - and you're safe.*

He tossed the pillow aside and dropped his arms onto his stomach. Still anxious, he took several deep breaths, and began to calm himself. He listened intently, could not hear the late-night insects sang their songs. In fact, there was no sound at all. It felt like the world was trying to tell him something had invaded stalking him.

The soft moonlight cast elongated grey shadows of the tree outside his window across the room. His heart stuttered, thinking the creature had gotten in. But that wasn't possible. Or, was it?

Gathering what was left of his courage, he turned his head towards the window. He gasped. It stood wide open. Fear all but froze him to the mattress. Thomas determined to overcome his terror and regain control of the night. He only wanted to return to sleep--peacefully.

Rolling to his side, he sat up and placed his feet on the floor. As he lifted himself off the bed, his eyes locked onto the open window. His knees buckled when two shadowy-black hands appeared at the top of the window. Two elongated feet sat on the windowsill and the toes rested flat on the faded wooden floor. His head jerked as he tried to get his mind to understand what he was seeing. Those clawed hands and long arms were a part of his nightmare.

But he was awake.

Terror choked off his breath as two leathery ears came into view followed by a bald forehead. Slanted, yellow eyes peered into the room, pulling a slight whimper from his seized lungs.

The creature continued to lower itself until its solid black form squatted on the window's ledge. Its arms now folded across its chest. It opened its mouth, filled with huge pointed teeth that dripped drool into a puddle on the floor. It reminded Thomas of cartoon characters from years past. Only this wasn't funny.

He broke out in a sweat and shivered uncontrollably as he stared directly into its eyes. Trapped.

The creature tilted its head from side to side, studying him. The shadow being didn't move, except for blinking from time to time.

It knows I'm awake. Please God, let it decide this is not the room it wants. Leave. Just leave.

He licked his dry lips as his hands searched for a shield … his blanket. They were out of reach, he had no protection … no safety.

I closed and locked the window. How did that thing get it open?

Now, it was too late to run.

Uncrossing its arms, the creature leaned on its knuckles and hobbled across the room in an ape-like manner. Less than five feet from the bed, it stopped and sat down once again.

If he could just get his legs to work and run to the bedroom door, maybe he could escape. After all, it's only a dream.

He sat and rocked back and forth on the edge of the bed.

The creature stood, mimicking his movements. With a glance at the door, it shook its head and smiled. "Oh Tommy, whatever am I going to do with you?" it asked in a high-pitched, sing song voice. "Did you think you could escape me by moving to a land of darkness and hiding in your bed?"

Thomas fell back on the bed. What in the seven worlds is this thing?

Affronted by the chastisement, Thomas said, "This isn't a land of total darkness - there's also twilight. And the moon and stars shine during full night. During the day, the sky is overcast and appears to be early evening for twelve hours." He crossed his arms over his chest and lifted his chin like a petulant child. "Besides, this place is easy on my eyes and nerves."

The creature clicked its tongue on the roof of its mouth. "Tommy … Tommy … Tommy. You can run, but you can't hide … especially from yourself." It taunted. "Let's return home now. Time has stopped for you, but it won't last forever."

Thomas turned his head toward the creature. "What makes you think I would leave the safety of my bed, the quiet of this world and a life I enjoy only to return to some world where there are monsters like you. For all I know, this is a trap and I'll become dinner for your family should I return."

"By the gods of Telstar, you are an idiot." The creature's voice held a tinge of annoyance. "I can't believe you don't recognize your own shadow." The shadow moved his hand to indicate his entire being. "Without you, I have no actual form. I'm forced to be this specter … something from nightmares. I am a part of you and you of me."

Thomas considered the being for a moment, then shook his head. "Sorry, I'm not convinced. A shadow is a shadow. It's attached to every solid object and follows that object everywhere."

The creature face palmed and scrubbed its claw down its face. Its shoulders drooped as it glanced about the room. Its eyes widened and a smile appeared as a notion dawned in its dark mind. It straightened and faced him. "Tommy, look around. Do you notice anything missing?"

Thomas cast about. His pocket contents still lay spread out on the dresser. The nightstand held his alarm clock and a half empty glass of water. The bed was obviously there as he was sitting on it. Throw rugs, wall posters, dirty clothes on the floor. Everything seemed to be right where he left when he crawled into bed.

Frustrated, Thomas growled at the creature. "I hate pop quizzes and I'm not a mind reader."

The entity sighed wearily.

Thomas snapped. "If you've got a point, then make it otherwise, go away and let me get back to sleep."

It picked up a book from the dresser. "Tommy, day or night, in this realm, there isn't enough light to cast a true shadow." Holding the book in the weak light the creature turned it from side to side. "Look. No true shadow."

Thomas pointed to the form on the floor, "What's that—a stain?"

"Granted, there is a greyish shape of the book, but no true shadow. A shadow requires light."

Thomas's momentarily forgotten fear came slamming back when the creature moved toward him. In a panic, he yanked his feet off the floor and stuffed them under his covers. "Don't touch me," he yelled at the beast.

It sat at the foot of the bed, inches from his feet. Thomas curled into a fetal position as his breathing reached the point of hyperventilation.

"Look, kid," the shadow tried to explain. "You've been lulled here with a feeling of false security. You are a creature of the light and you need to return to the light."

Thomas shook his head.

"And you need me, too. I am the one companion that will never leave you. I will always be there," it crooned, stretching a hand toward his human.

Thomas pulled himself in tighter.

"Tommy, without me, you aren't complete."

It spread his open hands, encompassing Thomas. "Even Peter Pan knew he needed his shadow. If you insist on staying apart from me it won't be long before you won't even be able to get out of bed. You will fade to nothing more than a forgotten memory. You will be a nothing."

Thomas considered that statement. He had heard of 'nothings'. They were people and things long forgotten and eventually no memory of them could be found. He shut his eyes to clear his thoughts.

Shadow seized the opportunity. Kicking his feet forward he attached them to Thomas. The young man's eyes sprung open, he pushed out his hands to remove the specters touch, but Shadow attached himself to the palms.

Quick as a flash, Shadow rolled towards the window. They were locked together with Tommy off balanced and unable to regain control. The two bounced against the wall and up onto the windowsill.

"OK, kid, there's no place like home." Shadow tipped them out of the window. They fell until they re-entered a world of light.

Thomas dropped onto his bed, landing like a ton of bricks. The mattress fought back and bounced Thomas right out of the bed.

Bright, yellow, morning sunlight shined through his window. The various colors of the walls, furniture and his night shirt hurt his eyes for a moment. He stood with his back to the window and looked at his feet. Relieved, he did a little dance to ensure his shadow was once again where it belonged. Attached to him … and only him.

Thomas felt whole again. He was safe from becoming nothing.

What a dream. Dreams within dreams within dreams.

When Thomas turned to the window, his shadow fell behind him. He didn't see his stretched shadow nod its head twice as a thought passed through his mind.

He isn't much, but he is mine.

4

KILLER CAMPING TRIP

IT HAD BEEN A WONDERFUL DAY. Don, Harvey, and I arrived at the Joshua Tree National Park in the San Bernardo National Forest. It was a crisp March morning, at just a little past nine and the temperature was around fifty degrees. Comfortable for us, but cool enough to keep the weekend warriors out of this section of the wilderness.

We followed a deer trail deep into the forest and found a clear stream just before noon. It sat at the bottom of a small plateau between two small mountains to our east and west, and a tall rocky challenge we didn't want to conquer.

The rise was level and dry, with plenty of firewood laying on the ground.

"I say we set up camp here and call this home until tomorrow afternoon," said Harvey. "Nice level ground with few rocks to embed themselves when we sleep." Harvey commented spreading his arms out toward the plateau. "There should be plenty of fish in that stream."

Rob and I agreed. Resting a bit, we embraced the beauty and solitude in our area. Rob and I took a few deep breaths and signed with the fresh smell of the wilderness. No exhaust, people shouting, and no noise except for the local wildlife. Between the various mountain peaks, the clear, blue sky stretched on for miles. The fast-flowing stream sat fifty yards from where we stopped.

For over a month, this trip had been all we all three guys talked about. A weekend of fishing and drinking.

We each carried a twelve pack of beer in our packs. Harvey's first order of business was to fill his extra fishing net full of the cans and drop them into the frigid water.

"They should be cold in about a half hour, just enough time for us to get the tents up, wood for the fire, and lines in the water." Harvey said.

Avid campers, it didn't take long for us to convert a small patch of dirt into 'home'. Don finished setting up his tent and stuck his head out, laughing at us. "I was just thinking, do we think that's enough beer to hold us for two days?"

"It had better be." Harvey said, "I sure don't plan on walking three hours to the car, find a store, and climb back up here. Of course, we could always take off and stay at a commercial camp site and drink beer and say we fished."

"That could happen. We wouldn't be the first guys to do something like that just to get out of the house." I laughed. "Now I wonder why we came all the way out here."

Harvey turned serious, "This is my annual get-a-way. But if you want to have the life of Riley for two days, it's simple. We take pictures of us with a couple fish, the scenery and camp site as alibis for the wives. All we need to do is change the dates on our cameras and take pictures this afternoon. We take more shots on Saturday, then change the dates on the camera to read Sunday. When we are packed up and ready to leave, we change the cameras go back to real time."

Don spoke up, "Just like visiting Vegas … no matter what we do, we can never talk about this trip. I for one don't want to experience the wrath of my wife, and no doubt you two want to live in peace at home."

Harvey finished the thought. "Since you two are tagging along, the rule is 'what happens camping - stays at the campgrounds."

Don stared at his friend, "It sounds like you've done something like this before, buddy. Want to share a story over the campfire tonight?"

Harvey shrugged his shoulders. Without saying another word, he grabbed his tackle box and rod as he walked down to the river.

Left with unfinished jobs, Don and I finished setting up. We also built the fire pit and gathered enough wood to last until morning.

Don was setting up his chair and other personal items. I waved and headed to the river.

I found Harvey sitting at the end of a log, his line in the water. He must have been daydreaming as he stared across the river.

I tapped him on the shoulder, and he jumped. So deep in thought he didn't hear me coming. "Wake up big guy, your line is moving. Looks like you caught dinner."

He reeled in the fish. It was at least a three-pound bass. "Well, it's a start. We need a couple more about this size to round out the day."

Don joined us as the fish went on the stringer. "Yeah man, this is your lucky day. One or two more and we can eat early, and return to civilization … after pictures of course." He said grabbing three beers out of the net, passing them around.

Harvey shook his head, "Yeah, my lucky day. I've now taken a fish away from its family. The big bad men are going to cook and eat as many as they can catch." He laughed, that quiet type of sound when you know something while everyone else wonders what is going on.

He had nothing else to say, so we spaced ourselves far enough apart as not to get our lines tangled yet remained within comfortable talking distance.

There was mundane chit chat between Don and me. Harvey sat at the far end of the natural bench, brows furled and as silent as a man at the top of a tree with zombies walking under him. We hoped Harvey would open up and tell us what was wrong.

"OK, man … fess up. What's going on?" I asked.

Don nodded, "Yeah. You're always the life of the party yet here you sit acting like the guy with a wife, girlfriend and car payment all two months late."

"What do you think Rob," Don laughed. "Debra kick him out and the tent is his new home?" He paused and looked at Harvey, "Or is your girlfriend demanding you get a divorce and marry her?"

Harvey stared at the ground. "No man. Sitting here reminded me of South America." We didn't hear his final comment as his voice became a mumbled whisper.

He reached into the net, pulled out a couple beers and headed up hill to the camp site.

"That must be a hell of a story." Don said. "What do you think Rod, could he have gotten hooked on that high-quality weed they grow down there?"

I stared at my friend for a few seconds before speaking. "Either that or something happened, and it is still eating at him. It's been fifteen years since he was in South America. PTSD eats away at a person until they can't stand life anymore."

Harvey returned to the stream and cast a line into the water. We fished in silence for another couple hours. The fish were biting, and we had more than enough for our fishing trip photographs and supper.

"Let's get pictures now." I suggested. "Then that job will be done and we can enjoy the rest of our weekend."

We took a series of pictures of each of us then group pictures by setting cameras on the log.

We caught enough that we took a second set using tomorrow's and Sunday's date and time, we faced a different direction to change the light.

"We're set." I said. "We can stay until early afternoon or leave in the morning."

We cleaned our fish on the edge of the water and put them in a plastic bag I always carry when fishing. Don grabbed a round of beers before we headed up the hill to cook our meal. Thanks to freeze-dried foods we always carry on trips as well as for camping and hunting, we would have a full dinner.

We sat around the campfire, even though it wasn't quite dark. The evening chill was starting to settle down from the mountains, but the comradery plus the beer, kept us warm and mellow. We talked about our time in the military, our families and of course sports.

We took turns going down and getting beers … no more than one each for the trip to help our favorite drink last until we went to bed.

The sky changed to a bright red making the clouds almost glow along the mountains. The sun dipped behind the mountains, turning its higher elevations from a growing grey to black.

"It will be dark soon. We should prepare dinner while it's still light." Don said.

Harvey assembled the cooking rack and put it over the fire. He heated the water for our side dishes and placed fish on the oversized frying pan near the fire. Reaching into his tent, he pulled out an insulated bag and poured out the ice and water, catching a package wrapped in aluminum foil before it touched the ground. He placed the package on the top rack and the bags of dried foods in the now boiling water.

"I'll put the fish on when the bags are ready to put on our plates. It won't take the fish but minutes to cook."

I went to the river and pulled six cans of bear from the net. Experience told me that we would drink more with our meal.

I handed everybody two cans and sat mine by my chair. I was in no hurry to pass out before we ate and heart Harvey's story.

It was turning dark, shadows disappeared as the campfire glowed brighter. Leaning forward on his stool, Harvey swallowed the last of his beer, stood and headed down to get another round. He was several cans ahead of me, but I wasn't counting.

He offered me a can, I held up my hand saying no thanks. He kept the second can and sat back on his stool.

Harvey seemed to have aged twenty years as he looked at Don and me. Dark circles, baggy, hound dog eyes, slacked jawed and pale faced, he spoke. "I know you are wondering about my comment this afternoon," he said soberly. "It's best I tell you the story before dinner. I wouldn't want you to be too upset to eat the fish, or swallow something abhorrent to you."

Don and I turned to each other, eyes wide and slack jawed waiting for the story.

Harvey paused and turned the package on the grill before shifting on his stool, looking directly at us.

"We were a squad of five elite special forces grunts, part of a multi-service taskforce traveling through the jungles finding various drug lords and their farms. Our job was to destroy the farms and terminate the dealers, growers and if we could find them, the drug lords with extreme prejudice." He finished his beer and opened the second.

With that brief comment, we were hooked. No one left the fire. Rob leaned forward and pulled the skillet on the top rack with his package.

"We were into the last two weeks of our six-month tour

when we stumbled on this village. It ran along a river similar to this. There were a half dozen huts 'horse-shoed' around the bank. Behind the huts there must have been a couple hundred acres of poppy plants."

He downed the rest of his beer, dropped the empty can, and stared at his feet. Raising his head, he continued. "Anyway, we crossed this river somewhere around the bend, out of sight. There were several old women on the bank, scrubbing their clothes. They hadn't seen us yet. They looked friendly."

He took several large gulps from the can. "Three members of the team split off to scout the field nearest to the village. There were older men and some children and teens harvesting the poppies, while young women hoed weeds in the neighboring section."

He looked around. I handed him my extra beer. He nodded his head in thanks and continued.

"The old ladies spotted us, and we were welcomed into the village, offering fresh water and fruit as we talked about the fields, the village and their daily life." He paused as he looked out towards the stream now covered in darkness.

"We are slaves to the patroon." One of the old crones said. "We never leave the village. They bring fresh food once a month or so. Not enough to keep everyone filled and strong."

"In English we debated our orders. Killing drug lords was one thing but wasting a village of poor, overworked people forced to serve the masters was another."

Another old woman added, "We must obey, or they take one of us down river, cut them so they bleed, and feed them from a boat to the piranha." Her voice broke in a sob, "They force us to watch."

In frustration, Harvey shook his fist in the air. Standing, he went down to get another round of beers. When he returned, his temper had cooled. He was relaxed, his hands no longer in fists and his face no longer beet red. He passed out the drinks and reclaimed his seat before he continued his story.

"A column of smoke rose from the middle of the field. The women explained it was their 'kitchen'. They had been serving the village from that spot for generations. We were invited to eat with them and talk to the men."

Harvey shook his head as though trying to clear his thoughts. "I've never talked about those last days, not even in my written reports. It's too disturbing, even now."

He paused and took several gulps of beer. "Evening approached," he whispered, staring into the fire. "We noticed the men, young women and children coming back to the village. We decided to gather as much intel as possible. We hadn't made up our minds, but our thoughts were to let the villagers live and leave this particular field alone. Experience taught us when we set fire to the plants, the village attacks. These people had opened their homes to us and they were slaves, not people of power. There was no need to kill."

Our attention was glued to Harvey and his story as he ran his fingers through his hair, as he rocked back in forth.

"As it turned dark, four men carried a large cast-iron pot between two posts to the center of the village. They threw dried sticks on the small fire until the flames increased, and then they added branches. They placed the pot in the middle of the flames. Introductions were made and everyone sat down to eat."

He paused, looking at his package. "One young woman ran through the group. As she glanced at the pot, went from crying to uncontrollable sobs. Bent over with shoulders slumped, she tripped, but she managed to stumble her way into a hut." He closed his eyes, his body shuttered as he shook his head. "She looked defeated ... as though her heart was broken. She did not come out to enjoy the meal."

Harvey paused as he turned his package on the rack and placed the fish back on the flame.

"It was a tasty stew. There was plenty of meat and a variety of local vegetation, grasses and who knows what floating in our bowls. We all had to admit, it beat MRE's."

His eyes glassed over, face blank, leaving us and reliving this memory. His eyes refocused before he spoke. "The locals relaxed and told us freely about their lives. They explained how the patroon had killed most of the game in the area. His men would invade the village and take their vegetables from the gardens. They managed to hide some under bad mats or in the brush, but his army always found most of the food. They even gave us directions to their patroon's palace."

Harvey stood, abruptly, knocking over his stool, and stomped to the bank once again. He returned with three more beers from the water. "We're almost out." He commented. "Guess we'll go home in the morning and make some pit stops along the way." He dropped the cans at his feet.

"We misunderstood when the women said they had been serving their people for generations." His voice snarled in anger as he opened the beer. Foam dripped down the can, covering his fingers. He studied the foam and lowered his head. "We were all enjoying the meal ... that is until one of the older boys went to the pot for seconds. He tripped and dumped it over."

Harvey smiled, he almost laughed as he remembered the accident. "The villagers didn't care that the boy was burned by the cauldron, the boiling stew or the fire. They were angry that the meal was poured on the ground and the fire drowned."

His face paled in the moonlight. "As the stew flowed toward the beach, we saw a child's head and a small hand flow a few feet in the sand and stop near us." He closed his eyes and shook his head, "At first we didn't move, until the yelling of the villagers snapped us out of our shock."

Harvey turned white and his hand shook so bad that he sloshed beer all over the ground.

Rob and I didn't have time to react to his story as we jumped up to catch Harvey before he fell to the ground. He recovered in seconds and straightened up on his stool.

"Sorry, the initial shock of what we saw still affects me today."

He took a deep breath and looked up at the sky. "The natives thought nothing of what had been in the caldron but yelled at the boy for spilling the meal. At first, the boy was surprised by his accident, but comments made by the adults must have scared him because he ran into the jungle. My guess was since he wasted food, it would be his turn in the pot tomorrow.

"We sat in shock for several seconds and stared at the hand as the liquid soaked into the sand. As one, we stood, pulled our Glocks and killed every man, woman and child. I stumbled to the hut with the woman. She was sprawled across a grass cot, crying. She rolled on her elbow and looked at me and bowed her head.

Tears flowed down her cheeks. "My son." She whimpered, "My son cooked in pot. He all I had. Please kill me, let me join him."

Harvey picked up his beer and stared at it. He placed it back in the sand without taking a drink.

"I ended up being the only one able to keep the meal down. The next morning, we burned the fields and made our way to the patroon's villa."

Harvey sneered. "We went in like a giant killing machine. We didn't hesitate to shoot any living soul we came across. We searched the mansion, every nook and cranny. In the end, we cornered the drug lord, his wife and child hiding in a storage building. We tied the adults to posts and prepared a special dinner for them. The teen age daughter didn't cry, scream, or beg for mercy. We slit her throat. Both parents' cries for mercy echoed across the villa as we cut her up and threw her parts in the pot."

His smile turned as cold as granite. "I explained to them that a village had been serving their children for generations in order to survive. The two parents should experience the same loss as their child was served as their final meal." He glared at Don and me.

We stared back —shell shocked.

Harvey continued. "After they ate, we gut shot them in the liver and let them bleed out a slow death. We set fire to all the buildings and walked away."

Tears flowed down Harvey's cheeks, "The other four guys couldn't live with what had happened, so they killed themselves before we were pulled out. I lied and said they were killed in the firefight at the drug lord's villa. "It's been years since that eventful day by the river. I relive that memory every day."

He lowered his head. "There is only one problem." He paused, looking up with a sad but guilty smile, "I still have a taste for it. I fight it as long as I can but every so often … I just can't stop myself. That's why I always camp alone in the spring."

With a gloved hand, he removed his package off the rack. Using his 'Rambo' knife, he put the fish out of the skillet and placed them on two plates. "You guys can have the fish," he said. Eyes sparkling as though he was possessed, his lips upturned into a small grin … "or join me."

He opened the wrapper, displaying the smoked torso of a small child. "I've been serving myself children after I gave up fighting the urge thirteen years ago."

Rob dropped his plate and began to gag. Standing, he rushed toward the underbrush away from our campsite. I could hear the beer splashing on some rocks. He returned to the campsite and staggered to his tent. I wondered how he would act in the morning after laying awake all night thinking about the story. I, on the other hand, dumped my fish into the fire and held my plate out for a slice of Harvey's other white meat."

5

KITTY GIFTS

IT ISN'T easy living in a city apartment that doesn't allow pets when you are a person who cares for every living creature. I can't bring them into the house, but there is no rule that says I can't take care of them outside. I put out a saucer of milk and some dry food for my neighbor's cat every morning.

My back patio faces the alley and back yards of single-family homes. When a dog runs away from home, or a cat goes on an adventure, they usually end up at my door, knowing food and attention is plentiful.

I always have treats, a kind word and scratches behind the ears or belly rubs for the wandering adventurers. After a short time, word spread across the block behind me and several owners would call to see if I had seen their "Charlie", "Spot", or "Thor".

As word spread, I became a household name. Several families would ask me if I could check on their homes and 'baby sit' their four-legged children when they were gone for a day or more. I loved taking them for walks or watching them play in a fenced yard.

One neighbor lived alone and despised his pet. "The creature is a fleabag. As far as I am concerned, she can drink from the creek, catch, and eat local wildlife. I wish she was out of my life."

I am sure she had her share of mice, squirrels, and rabbits.

I wondered why he adopted the lovely and affectionate female tabby that he left out to fend for herself in any kind of weather.

She had a quiet way about her, always loving and seeking attention. We adopted each other and I feel better for 'Kitty' when she gets a bit of milk and appropriate food every day.

Since I can't keep her in the apartment, I fixed up a wooden box with straw and a blanket in the winter to help keep her warm. When it snows, I hang a light in the box for added heat and make sure she always has extra food and water.

"Kitty" doesn't go up to the old man's house anymore, I am her family. When she hears my sliding glass door open, she will scamper across the alley, or charge out of the field on the side of my apartment for a snack. And in the evenings, she joins me as I sit in my chair with a drink to read or watch the sunset.

Our relationship has changed a bit in recent weeks. Since I am now her family, she shows how much she loves me by bringing me thank you gifts, or perhaps it is some sort of payment in the hopes I would allow her to move into my home. Deep inside, I think she is afraid she will be abandoned once again.

I have received such gifts as bones from the dumpster, a dead or dying mouse, pieces of partially eaten fast food in torn wrappers. I always thank her and scratch her ears and remind her that the gifts aren't necessary for our arrangement. However, I can't allow her in the apartment.

This morning, I opened my sliding glass door and watched Kitty scamper out of the woods. She held something unusual in her mouth. I wasn't sure, but it looked like a small, shiny doll, perhaps a GI Joe action figure or some other toy. When she reached me, she dropped her gift in front of my chair. After placing her paw on the prize, she looked up and 'asked' for her breakfast with a small meow.

"What do you have for me today, Kitty?" I asked as I knelt down and placed her two bowls off to the side.

She looked at me with searching eyes then walked over to her treats, leaving the doll at my feet. Imagine my surprise when the six-inch toy, dressed in a silver jump suit rolled over, sat up and stared at me with big round eyes.

"My name is Alana, I come in peace." She said with a soft, almost erotic voice that made my jaw drop. "I mean no harm and will grant you great rewards if you help me."

Unable to speak, I nodded and sat back in my chair. A million questions flew through my mind, but I was unable to vocalize a single thought. I shook my head to help return me to reality and examined the diminutive woman before me.

On close inspection, I estimated her height to be around five and a half to six inches. She had curves in all the right places, long black hair, large expressive eyes, and her voice … God, it held just the right tone than stopped me in my tracks.

She stood, never taking her eyes off mine. The silver suit covered her from neck to somewhere inside the matching boots. It was obvious to me that she was studying me as much as I her.

"You are a giant of a race. This is not what our intelligence sources provided." She said, "Obviously, mistakes have been made, or perhaps I am simply on the wrong planet. I did have some navigation problems along the way."

Her English was eloquent. "You're a space alien." I stuttered, "Not some new animatronic doll?"

She laughed. "I am no doll," she said. "I am a living being from a planet in the Tadpole galaxy in the Draco constellation. As you can see our people are quite small. I have traveled over twelve hundred light years to this planet only to find that our settlement fleet has gone elsewhere."

"Does this mean your people invaded this planet eons ago?" I asked.

She nodded. "At the time of their departure, this planet showed no intelligent life. Our plan was to send a group of settlers to terraform this world, then send others. When we received no word, my ship was sent to determine what had happened."

"You know, twelve hundred light years is even more earth years and it is possible that your people landed here before the human race had evolved and have either moved on or died out."

She tilted her head in thought. "Yes, I guess that is possible." She said. "This planet has gone through many changes. I noted many destructions of the surface while traveling through space. There have been multiple life forms and civilizations, but I thought it was our people growing and spreading over the entire world. I have no idea what to do next,"

"If your ship can fly, why don't you return home?" I asked.

Again, she seemed to think through my question. Her hand held her chin; once again her head tilted to the side, hair flowed down her shoulders almost to her waist. At long last, she looked up and said, "I would need to find supplies and a source of fuel, provided it is available on this planet. Thanks to the violent entry in the atmosphere, the ship needs a bit of cleaning up and minor repairs on the exterior, but it can fly."

She studied me for a few minutes. "I have a proposal for you ... If you will allow me to bring my ship here and reside in your dwelling. I can provide you with knowledge that would allow you to become rich and acquire whatever you desire for happiness."

Although I doubted she held any power over the universe that would allow me to find quality work or teach me ways to improve my life, I agreed to allow her to move in and I would help her in all ways possible to repair her ship and return home.

"Please allow me to examine your living quarters. We need a certain amount of space to keep my craft as well as lay out the various parts for repair."

Alana walked towards the door. As she stepped on the threshold, "Kitty" pounced and batted her out of the doorway. Claws bared and growling, she snatched Alana by the head and neck. When Kitty bit down, Alana's scream ended abruptly, kitty dropped Alana to the patio. Blood flowed from Kitty's mouth, landing in resonating plops on the concrete. My loving cat quickly devoured the alien's remains.

"Kitty, what have you done?"

I collapsed in my chair. Now, I will never know if Alana could have brought me riches and happiness.

Since then, I have taken up hiking in my free time, especially exploring the wooded areas around the neighborhood. Alana couldn't have traveled far as Kitty tends to stay close to home. And, she did not say she traveled alone. If I could find her ship, I may find another survivor. If her people came here and survived, perhaps I can become a haven for a long-forgotten race.

In the meantime, I still have "Kitty" and who knows what she may find for me tomorrow.

6
———

TOGETHER

Alex sat beside the hospital bed and held her hand. He no longer heard the beeps and signals from the various machines along the wall. He ignored the tubes inserted in her nose and mouth. He whispered all the things he had failed to tell her during their forty-five years together.

He watched her as the various monitors and medical equipment keeping her bodies activity and medical equipment kept her alive. It was no secret she was alive but had no life, no thoughts or responses to her surroundings. She was nothing but a being, they kept breathing by the equipment surrounding her.

"Piper, my love, I wish I had told you every day how much I love you and how you have made me a better man. I should have helped you around the house, taken you on all the trips we talked about for the honeymoon we never had, and I am so sorry we never had children."

Her chest rose and fell to the digital tempo of the machines. Tears tracked down his cheeks, as he thought about how they had grown together and now forever apart.

His mind was filled with guilt … it was all coming to an

end … in all the years they were together he only kept two big secrets from her.

He was aware she couldn't hear him, but he had to clear his conscience, and let her know … he knew. For five years … he knew.

There had been no brain activity for several days. She lay in the bed like a ragdoll. There were times he wondered if he closed the curtain and made love to her, would she respond. It would have been his final act of defiance, but he feared getting caught and knew the staff would kick him out of the hospital.

"Piper, today's the day. If you don't move … don't respond in some way, the doctor is going to disconnect everything. You will die.

I can't live without you knowing what I have known for years and how I continued to love and worship you." He laid his head on her chest, not quite crying, but filled with remorse and sadness.

Doctor Fields entered and placed his hand on Alex's shoulder. "I need you to sign the forms for organ donation, son. We will begin in about ten minutes. At first, you won't notice any change. In seven minutes, we will hook a stimulator and monitor that will keep her heart beating enough to keep everything viable. We will take her to surgery and begin the surgeries for transplants with whatever organs are viable. The donors are already in the surgical suites here and in other hospitals across town.

Alex straightened in the chair and focused on Dr. Fields. "I understand. Give me the clip board and I'll sign whatever you need. All I ask is that you let me stay until you wheel her out."

"If that is what you want. Please stay."

Handing the clipboard back to Dr. Fields, he asked, "When can I see her. Her clothes are at the mortuary, her hair is short and won't take much to fix."

"We have called the mortuary. They will pick her up after the harvest. You can visit with her after they have her placed in the viewing room. You can go around seven this evening. I made all the arrangements for you to get in."

Alex simply nodded, Dr. Fields stopped at the door and turned back. "The nurse will come in and disconnect everything except the heart monitor in a few minutes. I will tell the staff to let you stay until they take her to surgery."

Several minutes later, Nurse Angela entered the room. "I'm so sorry Alex, I know you two have had a long, loving life together."

He smiled, just enough to thank the nurse, and watched as she began turning off alarms and removing tubes from her body. One by one, the various monitor's numbers went to zero.

"I'll give you a chance to say your final goodbyes. I'll be back in a moment."

When Angela left the room, he leaned over into his wife's ear. "You know Piper, I knew about all your affairs. I forgave you because you always took care of me. With our twenty-year age difference, I understood you had needs I couldn't fulfill. The key was you took care of me first."

His hand caressed her cheek. "Then, two years ago, you began to ignore me. When you began go out more often. His face flushed with anger. "I followed you one night and discovered you had found a very young man. "Alex shook his head in disbelief, "I could handle the age difference between you two, but not that you chose to give me up for him."

Anger continued to seep into his voice. "I vowed revenge … not on him, but on you. You broke my heart."

His hand fisted into her sheet. "First I used small amounts of rubbing alcohol in your eye drops. Over time, you lost your vision. I gave you several months to finish with the various eye doctors, Yet, not one of them could stop the inevitable. Permanent blindness. The loss of your sight made it impossible for you to go out and cheat on me. But, that didn't solve the real problem." His fingers stroked her lips, then traveled down her body.

"You expected, no demanded me to be your care giver with no reward." He smiled, "Ah but I got even. When you refused my advances, I moved on to my next plan. I was able to buy Botox on the black market. You know, the stuff that cures migraines and takes the wrinkles out of your skin ... well I fed a few drops to you every few days. Within months, you got weak and sick. Now here you are ... at death's door."

He raised his head and looked at her once more. Despite all this, I still love you, with all my heart. We will see each other again in the afterlife. I am guessing we will be together in hell."

Angela entered the room. "Time to go, Alex," She said putting her arm over his shoulder.

Alex started to rise, then fell back into the chair, head bowed, sobbing for the loss of his loving wife. "Can I sit a while? Give me ten minutes to gather my strength after you take her. A nurse can get me. I know you have to save lives with her organs."

"Doctor Fields said if you asked, you could stay until we wheel her out to surgery. The operating room is almost ready for her. I have to go get the aides. I'll be right back."

A short time later, Angela returned with two men. They placed Piper on the gurney and left the room. "I'll come back and get you in a few minutes." She said.

Head still slightly bowed, and sobbing, Alex gave a vague nod and stared up at the blank monitors. after they unlocked the gurney, one of the aides turned the power off.

Alex sighed. Piper, his life ... his love. His selfish wife was gone.

Alex couldn't see a world with him wondering alone. He could not allow his beautiful Piper to travel down death's road alone. He pulled a folded piece of paper from his jacket pocket and placed it on the bed. Large block letters read "TO WHOM IT MAY CONCERN".

It gave the hospital the right to use any and all organs. He stated he could not live without her and he would die where her life had ended.

From the other pocket of his wind breaker, he clutched a pocketknife. He flicked open the razor-sharp blade.

Taking a deep breath, he drove the blade into the bend of his shoulder under his left underarm and forced the blade down his arm to the wrist. He stared at the crimson liquid pooling on the floor.

He leaned his head against the back of the chair, closed his eyes. Piper stood before him, her arms outstretched, welcoming him on the journey to eternity.

Nurse Angela entered the room saying "Alex, it's time for you to…."

She yelled down the hall, "I need a doctor, we have an attempted suicide in 305."

Doctor Fields rushed into the room. There was no pulse and enough blood on the floor to show Alex had bled out and was gone. He found the note. "He's donated his organs, get him to surgery. Get tissue tests completed and contact patients."

Alex and Piper watched from above as they floated near the ceiling. He looked at his wife and smiled. They would not be separated. "I knew, all along, what you were doing. I never understood until you shut me out."

His voice was soft, but hard edged. "I killed you. But, I couldn't live without you … so I killed myself." He had an evil grin as his eyes squinted in hate for Piper.

He laughed when she gasped, "Now you will travel through eternity with me and you will do as I dictate."

A portal of bright light appeared through the wall. He squeezed her hand as they entered the new world. Staring into her husband eyes she whispered, "We'll see."

7

SOUL SUCKER

DILLON WANDERED around the amusement park for hours. The shows had been fun, but the rides were, for the most part, disappointing. They would spin, turn, climb and drop but nothing truly extreme that made his heart pound in his throat.

He did enjoy the food. The treats were the real reason he had come to the carnival. Once a year, he broke his diet. Traveling three hours to the state park, he saw the shows, watched the people, but what made the trip worthwhile was the food. All those sweet and greasy treats that made him feel like a regular person. He would stuff himself with corn dogs, cotton candy and all the things he wasn't supposed to eat.

Although the rides were now mundane and held no adventure, he enjoyed watching the women as they came down the exit ramps … dizzy, confused and their hair all tangled. Their antics made him laugh and he had to admit, at times aroused.

Nearing midnight, the crowds thinned out, but Dillon continued to wander the park. He enjoyed his last corndog and coke as he walked the grounds deciding what he wanted to do next. I think I will have another funnel cake for desert and explore the park one last time to make sure I didn't miss anything.

He walked around the back of the rides, gaming booths and the big top just to see how things work behind the action. Dillon enjoyed the machinery. The smell of grease, gasoline, and diesel all mixed together brought back memories of truck servicing and repairs while in school. The clank of the hubs as they redirected and spun the rides kept rhythm with the gears and braces as they moved around and sideways. The noise was camouflaged by the loud music being played with each ride.

Taking a deep breath, he realized the smells of the equipment was hidden by the variety of scents from the frying foods throughout the grounds.

He continued his wandering to a row of gaming booths. He loved the ones using ropes to win a prize. They are all neat and easy to separate by the rube. The contestant would track a rope until it went above the curtain and try to figure out what prize it connected to. They would pull and be filled with disappointment when they didn't win their reward. Behind the curtains it was a whole new world. Various strings were tied together to the same prize and only a few of the bigger prized were attached to the winning cord. I can't believe the people would keep playing a no-win game.

I guess I should head for the gate, I have a three-hour drive home.

Checking his watch, he turned his head to avoid getting a face full of dirt between two tents when he spotted a glow farther back from the corner of the fairgrounds. The gentle pastel lights seemed to flicker as the gentle breeze and bordered along the fence at the end of the fairgrounds. I can't see what is behind the lights, and they are too far out to be a part of the fair. There is no construction equipment expanding the fairgrounds. Whatever is out there is sitting on private property. Squinting, whatever was there was farmland.

His curiosity wetted, he walked towards the light. Even though the evening had been enjoyable, he was still looking for one last great adventure.

He headed toward the distant lights in a mist. As he got closer, the mist turned to fog.

The area was covered in the soft glow of lights. There was silence … the hum of the machinery, the blaring music, nor the murmur of the remaining people or rides could make their way into this living curtain. Ignoring the growing fog, his pulse increased as he believed he discovered something new. He quickened his pace focused on the light shining.

He could barely make out the shape of what may be a building - silhouetted by the lights. The mist began to clear as he neared a cyclone wire fence. He touched the metal and the ride came into view. The mist evaporated, unveiling a new ride.

It had a spooky feel to it the outline of the building was similar to paintings of hell. There were creatures pulling humans apart or eating the bleeding limbs of children. Dillion's mouth hung open as the scene planted nightmares in his mind. He suspected the yellow lights hid the true color of the paintings on the buildings. In his heart, he knew it was blood red.

Perhaps it will be introduced for Halloween, but it is a bit graphic for a lot of families. I guess they could replace the old fun house with this, but it needs to be toned down a bit.

Two people were getting tickets as another couple walked to a waiting car. Dillon stood at the outer edge of the glow of the lights.

Stepping closer to the fence, he was surprised to see a clear plastic ticket booth. Swinging her feet inches above the ring on the stool, he realized she was a little person.

She gave the next couple their tickets and pointed to the car waiting on the track. As the pair strolled hand-in-hand to the ride, the lights grew brighter. As they sat bemused, his arms already around her shoulders. As they kissed, the mist surrounded them almost like a shroud.

The lights dimmed, Dillon, blinked ... the car disappeared and an empty one appeared in its place. There was no woosh or sound of machinery pulling the car through an unseen door.

Intrigued, Dillon studied the dimensions of the front of the building. He kept a safe distance and began walking along the length of the fence. The structure was small, perhaps the size of a double wide trailer. "At most, the car could only make one "U" turn to finish the ride, the structure doesn't extend to the outer wall of the building." He muttered to himself. "It can't be a 'fun house' there are no mechanical screams or sounds coming from the inside."

It was a rectangular construction that now looked like cut stone instead of wood. There were no extensions, or angles, that allowed to increase the length of the ride. It was far too small to provide much of a thrill.

Several feet of the fence, in front of the ride, was actually the end of the fairground. The ride extended beyond the fence, trespassing on farmland. The building smashed the stalks of corn growing in the field.

Deep in thought, he found himself standing outside the gate, staring at the ride. The young woman exited the ticket booth and walked to the gate.

He smiled at the young woman and said. "I am intrigued by your ride and wonder what all it has to offer."

"I noticed you. Not many people are that interested in how the Soul Sucker is constructed. You are a different breed of human." She responded.

Walking toward the woman, he realized, she was full grown, and no more than three and a half feet tall. She was a well-formed woman, and sensual for a little person.

"I was wondering if I could try out the ride." He said, "It

looks interesting, and I have never seen anything shaped like this attraction."

"I'm so sorry," she said, "This is a couple's or small group ride. It is also time to shut down and call it a night."

Disappointed, he eyes searched and took in every detail one last time at the ride. "Perhaps next year, then. I will come searching for you as soon as I arrive." He walked away.

"You know," she called out, "I could make you the last ride of the night." She scanned the field, "There's no one walking out to the ride from the fairgrounds and it's a rule of the ride, you can't travel alone, but I would be happy to sit with you so you can experience the thrill of the unknown. If you enjoy having your breath taken away, you will turn blue."

"Thank you" Dillon said, "but I've been on lover's rides before and it wouldn't be the same traveling with a stranger. Half the thrill is the intimacy."

"You will find this ride is more than a time for lover's to be alone in the dark. This is an adventure - an experience that will stay with you for a lifetime" She said latching the gate … her voice sent chills down his spine. Her laugh, like the cackle of the wicked witch of the west scratched on his nerves. It didn't match the smoothness of her speaking voice, but he overlooked the sound.

Her skin was flawless and had a softness that glowed in the haze filled light. Her full lips spread across perfectly even white teeth in an inviting smile. Her eyes beckoned him.

"You can put your arm around me, sit close and whisper your thoughts in my ear. And once you experience the ride, you will want to ride it over and over. Bring your girl next time or come late and I will ride with you again."

Dillon stepped toward the ticket booth, reaching for his billfold.

The woman waived her hand, "No charge. We are testing new ideas and all we ask is for everyone to share their experience of riding "The Soul Sucker". She waved her hand indicating for Dillon to follow her to the ride.

Dillon's five-foot, nine-inch frame had trouble matching her pace as her little legs ate up the ground.

Even if the ride were a bust, being with this woman while experiencing a new adventure, would make the time worthwhile. There was no false pretense. She was unlike any regular sized woman he had met.

Dillon had his doubts, but with this unusual woman beside him, the ride might be more exciting.

He climbed into the car and the sensual ticket agent jumped into the seat beside him. The fog surrounding the ride thickened until it blocked his view beyond the opened car. he could no longer see anything but the grey mist hiding the world.

His expectations of a thrilling ride plummeted when he couldn't find any seat belts or safety bars. So much for an exhilarating ride.

She lifted his arm, wrapped it around her shoulders, and snuggled close. "You're going to hold me tight in just a few seconds." She laughed.

They broke through the mist into a bright light. He was transported to another time and place. The car transformed from the open carriage into a flying carpet. There were no rails as they floated above the clouds until they broke into the afternoon sun among indescribable and beautiful mountains. Dillon's jaw dropped and his eyes widened. A valley appeared as the carpet descended into a valley filled with deep-green vegetation. A winding, red river flowed somewhere out of site.

As they continued, he peered over the edge of the carpet. Dinosaur like creatures of various sizes grazed in the valley below. Twice the size, some walked on four legs, others on two. A shadow as a ginormous, long-beaked bird flew above them.

He turned towards the woman to say something but

found his mouth was locked in an open position and rendered him speechless.

Her eyes glittered like a thousand candles as she soaked in the beauty. She reached over and closed his mouth. "You ain't seen nothing yet!" she whispered, then kissed him lightly on the lips. She stood between his legs and embraced him. The carpet folded in on itself and dropped like a boulder off the side of a plateau.

Dillon's stomach caught in his throat. The bright sunshine and magnificent sights disappeared in less than a heartbeat and he found himself surrounded in nothingness. It was as though someone had dropped him into the center of a cavern with no light. He at the side of the carpet, flinched when his hands met empty air.

She whispered into his ear. "Don't worry. It's only a thousand feet until we enter another dimension. It's a world from one of my favorite dreams. Your adrenaline is going to soar."

True to her word, they came to a sudden stop. Dillon slid forward, his stomach still in his throat. The woman's arms tightened and pulled him to her as she remained anchored where she stood. His stomach suddenly settled.

The carpet stood still for several seconds in the dark. When it crawled forward, the carpet converted into a flatbed wagon and it slid through the curtain of subdued light.

They had truly entered into a new dimension as Dillion found himself at some strange party where humans, creatures, and monsters were taking one another with total abandon. Shocked, they collapsed on the edge of the wagon. He watched in disgust and amazement as the beings were not only mating, but many were devouring the bodies of others. The living screamed and cried out for God to help them while the dead simply jerked, and the predators devoured flesh and drank the blood of their victims. Others fought each other over the body parts laying on the ground.

She leaned over and hugged Dillon, tight and sensual, "I get aroused every time I enter this dimension." She said. Her body rubbing his and her hands reaching inside his pants.

"Isn't it exciting," she said, leaning over the edge of the wagon.

Dillon watched as her arm reached over the side and touched human and monsters alike as the wagon passed by. "Here, touch something." She grabbed his hand and pulled it over the edge of the wagon. "They can't see us, but you will know what they are feeling and experiencing."

She continued to stroke the pelts of beasts and the backs, chests, organs of men and women. The partygoers would stop and look around trying to find what or who had touched them.

Dillon rolled to his hands and knees and stroked the mane of a lion-like creature. He felt the energy of the beast course through his body. He was suddenly alive with a variety of uncontrolled emotion. As he touched beings and humans, their passions and darkness filled him with haunting desires.

He touched a woman bent over servicing a giant of a man with pointed ears. Just as the world, once again, turned black, Dillion lost all control, he reached for the miniature woman with uncontrolled desire. The wagon entered the darkness, arriving at another destination. This time, he was able to see shapes around him.

He engulfed the woman in his arms and put his lips to hers. The kiss was filled with animal passion as they attacked one another. She bit his lip, her claw like nails ripped their way through his clothing, drawing blood. Filled with animal desires, he began tearing her clothing, biting and scratching her just to smell and taste her flesh and blood.

The wagon transformed into the car, he lowered her to the floor and took her as they entered another cavern. She wore nothing under the simple, short dress and arched her body in passion as his entered her.

The sound of screaming drew his attention, he stopped pounding the woman and peered out the full-length front glass of the car. She was oblivious to the sonds and continued bucking him with complete abandon.

It took a moment for his mind to grasp the scene before his eyes. They were catching up to the other car that had started the ride before them.

Though he closed his eyes, a bright red light filtered through his eye lids. He could see the blood spraying from the bodies of the two people ahead of them. He started to pull away, but she held onto him, impaling her body up to his.

Grabbing her waist with both arms, he managed to stand and sit on the padded cushion. She remained attached to him as she wrapped her short legs around his waist. Her head buried into his neck, biting hard enough to draw his blood.

Dillion tensed when her teeth entered his neck. Suddenly his mind and body filled with desire on steroids. He grabbed her head and pushed her head deeper into his shoulder. His body shook as she feasted on his blood.

Creatures, demons, devils, and monsters from the paintings on the front of the Soul Sucker relished as they pulled what was left of the riders from their car and continued to pull apart their bottom halves like pulling apart a wish bone at Thanksgiving dinner.

The howls and screams continued as the creatures fought over the remaining body parts of the former riders. They tossed any remaining parts of the bodies into a pit below as flames rose to lick their feet. Finished, they faded away.

Leaning forward, as the woman continued to ride him, he saw the souls of many people screaming from the pit. They were the bodies of thousands of people, yet not solid, but a mist, like that surrounding the ride. Dillon saw their spirits as he looked down. Other hellish creatures devoured or played with the spirits and ghostly bodies in the most depraved ways.

In a cold sweat and shaking with fear, Dillon fell back into the seat, certain he was the next person to be consumed.

The woman, still driving him into her body whispered in his ear.

"Don't worry, they won't hurt you. I, however, am another matter."

She shifted her weight as she remained attached to him, sitting on his lap grinding instead of bouncing up and down. "I told you this would be the thrill of a lifetime." She keened.

Her skin changed to scales the color of bright red and yellow found in a lava flow. "I like you. If you last until the end of the ride, there is a price, but I will let you live."

She bit into his neck a second time as her hips pounded against him. "I know what it takes to gain your soul." She whispered when she released his neck and took a breath.

Dillon's world returned to black. He felt her slide off his body and vaguely wondered how he had managed to remain in control. As the grey fog loomed in front of him, the woman dropped to her knees—her head covered his lap.

Teeth bit once more and sucked so hard he thought his very existence would flow out of his body.

They coasted into the land of eternal mist. He felt the car rise into the fog. Dillon slouched on the bench of the car – too weak to escape.

Opening his eyes, he discovered the woman sitting primly in her spot, holding his hand. They were fully dressed in unripped clothes with no signs of blood.

Dillon took a shaky breath and let it out slow. The ride was an illusion. The mist was some kind of a hallucinogenic drug that brought forth hidden desires and fears. There was nothing to fear.

With a smile she said, "I do believe you are impressed. I hope you will come back soon for another ride." She reached up and gave him a big hug. "Make sure you bring a companion."

She laughed that rough gravelly voice once more. "Choose your companion carefully … but don't worry, you will see me in your dreams."

Like a zombie, Dillon made his way out of the fairgrounds. He walked, through the parking lot until he found his car. One hand on the steering wheel, he absently looked at his watch. Only ten minutes had passed since he changed his mind and walked over to the Soul Sucker ride. His mind couldn't grasp how he had walked to the ride, experienced the adventure of his life, and arrived in the same length of time it took to walk to his car.

He cast about, looking for the Soul Sucker, but found only the empty field.

He was suddenly struck with the realization that he felt nothing. He searched deep within for any kind of emotion … surprise … fear … anger. It was all Gone. Empty.

The ride was not an illusion. In those last moments, the little person was the instrument that turned him into a hollow shell. The ride had sucked away his soul.

It was then he remembered her parting, fateful words, "You'll see me in your dreams."

8

UNSEEN

I AM AN INVISIBLE MAN. I wander the community unseen by those around me. It wasn't always like this. There once was a time when everyone noticed me.

In school, classmates, peers, and teachers knew me by sight and sound. I was full of life and active. I continued to grow in importance. Sandlot baseball was my favorite sport and always the one first to be on a team I was too small in stature for basketball, but I was fast and light on my feet, so I survived football as a receiver.

I became somewhat invisible during college, although everyone involved in my major and minor knew and interacted with me during this time. I realized that I was no longer a big fish in a small pond … I was now a small fish in an exceptionally large lake.

My career, if you want to call it that, allowed me to meet and mingle with a variety of people. I held positions involving small groups of underlings and being integrated with several hundred individuals in a department or company, depending on the position.

My invisibility occurred slowly … over many years. It

started simply enough, being overlooked when the waitress was providing coffee refills, ignored when trying to order a drink at a bar. I was ignored in simple things, like trying to involve myself in conversations. People just didn't see or hear me. It got to a point where I had to go out of my way to get any type of attention, which also gave me the reputation of being rude.

I faded from sight even more as I entered middle age, and now, I'm in my late fifties and no one notices me. There are times when it is a blessing. I am like the mailman. I travel from store to store, take what I want, and no one sees me. I can sit on a bench or a chair in a coffee shop and watch people walk by, always unnoticed. It is still frustrating, yet, I have found a new upside to my curse.

That is how we met, you know. I watched you for days, always in a hurry, never paying attention to your surroundings. You were enticing in your short skirts and tight pants, sleeveless blouses, and dresses with thin straps over your shoulders.

I stared at you, drooled with lust in my mind as you walked by, but you never noticed me. I moved each day, closer to your destination until I discovered where you worked, parked your car. Hell, I even followed you home and you never saw me.

The more I got to know you, the more I knew you were special. Bumping into you a couple of times, you looked right through me, not even a response.

When I touched you in the elevator, on multiple occasions, as we traveled to your floor at the insurance company, even when we were going down and I followed you to your special parking space at the end of the day, you remained unaware of me.

Yes, I was rude, but you were so high and mighty … so self-important, you didn't have time to notice all the liberties I took touching you. Wrapped up in your own selfish world, you ignored the regular people around and the special one ... ME.

That's why it was so easy ... you entered the parking lot. I waited a half an isle down from you until a spot opened and parked my van next to your car. I sat all day waiting for you to return. As usual, you walked alone. I recognized the click of your heels. My sliding door was unlocked, and I moved over so we would be next to each other. I waited, listening to all noise in the parking lot.

I knew no one could see me. My van was simply parked in a spot near you. As time grew close for you to arrive, I sat in the driver's seat and waited. It was my lucky day, the SUV parked on your driver's side pulled away. I pulled into that spot and waited.

I heard your keys jingle as you leaned over to unlock your car. It was so easy, I slid open the side door and smacked you in the head and put you on the floor of my van. With zip ties I made sure you couldn't use your arms or legs to try and escape as I drove you the hour to my farm.

With luck, no one will miss you until Monday. I removed my license plates, wore a mask and gloves. No one will see me, even if they try. Now you are mine ... mine to keep for as long as I like.

One thing is disappointing, you still don't see me. It is Sunday morning. You are wide eyed, and you scream from time to time. You appear surprised when food arrives in front of you. You continue to stare right through me.

"I guess you aren't as special as I thought. Time is up..." I say in sadness. "I thought you would take the time to open those sky-blue eyes and realize you weren't along."

Clutching a grapefruit spoon, I scan all my other disappointments along the walls. I look them all in the eyes, preserved in jars. "Watch this," I say to those who have come before you.

I pull back the eye lid and stare one last time in those

beautiful eyes that caught my attention so many months ago. I dig deep, spinning the spoon then holding the eyes in the spoon. We once again look eye to eye as I ask … "Can you see me now?"

9

LUNCH WITH THE DEVIL

THURSDAY and I was stuck in a meeting until well after lunch time. My choices—take my lunch break or leave work an hour early. My growling stomach made the decision for me. I hung my "out to lunch" sign on the outer corner of my cubicle wall and left the building.

The small eatery at the end of the block was all but empty. One homeless guy crouched at a small table in a dark corner trying to hide from the staff, a young couple staring into each other's eyes as they 'studied' by the front window and now me. I ordered the special, beef and noodles, salad and vegetable of the day, iced tea and water. I also ordered the same meal for the old man in the corner. I figured he could take the rest of the day to finish the meal.

I had just taken the first bite when a tall, thin man walked up to my table. He smiled, sat his brief case on the floor and settled into the chair across from me.

"Mind if I join you?" He asked with a voice sounding like gravel being dumped from a large truck.

"Guess not, since you've already made yourself at home." I replied and returned to my lunch.

He flipped open a pocket notebook and studied it for a

moment. "Robert Tidwell, 45, Executive Junior Partner at Rogers – Jackson – Anderson law firm, single - - never married." The man said. "Interesting, you are an Executive Partner and your office is a six by eight cubicle instead of a room."

I glanced up from my plate and studied the man sitting across from me. The stranger had a thin hawk-like face with a long-pointed nose, crow's feet dug a deep furrow at the corner of his ice blue eyes. "And just who the hell are you and what are you selling." I demanded.

The man's eyes lifted above the top of his notebook and smiled. His crooked teeth were filed to sharp points, resembling sharks' teeth. Ignoring the question, he continued, "You had one serious relationship during your four years at Yale, a Marianne Glockworth." He gave me a smirk and licked his lips in what seemed to be a sexual reflection of my old love. "You dated through your junior and senior years in college. The day of graduation she walked away and married your roommate, Dennis … something. He waved his hand dismissing Dennis, "He doesn't matter in our discussion."

I put down my fork. "Who are you and what are you selling?" My voice was short and bordering on anger. "It doesn't matter, I'm not buying. Please leave so I can finish my lunch."

"Why Mr. Tidwell, I'm The Devil and I am here with a proposition." He gave me a used car salesman smile. "I have the ability to make you the happiest man in the world."

I glared at the Devil before I picked up my fork and continued eating, "I'm happy and I'm not buying your insurance or whatever, please get lost." I dismissed this intruder and concentrated on my meal.

The Devil shrugged his shoulders, a look of shocked disbelief on his face. He must be used to those eager to take his deal and find out later there is a catch. I took a bite of my salad trying not to laugh. This guy did his research and thought I would be an easy mark. With a bit of checking, he would know I had pined for Marianne since the day she walked out of my life. Her decision cost me my one, true love and my best friend.

"Robert, you don't understand." He said breaking into my thoughts. "I am the Devil. Satan. Beelzebub." He spread his arms wide in an expression of his power. "I have the power to turn back the clock to the time before Marianne left you for … what's his name."

I managed to laugh and not spit half chewed food in his face by covering my mouth with my hand. "Man, you should take this show on the road, you are funny as hell."

He didn't give up. He continued as though he didn't hear me.

"If you sign a contract, you can begin your life over with the woman of your dreams. You would have the one thing you missed in life … a wife, kids, home with a white picket fence, everything you have wished for when you fell in love."

I glared at the intruder. "Go away and leave me alone. I am happy with my life … just the way it is." I paused, enjoying his frustration of not agreeing to his proposal. "I've got to admit, for a fallen angel, you have a good research team. You went back twenty plus years to work this scam."

The Devil face turned red and sweat broke out on his forehead. "Try to take me serious, Bob. This is not a scam. Look, I have a contact with me." He said taking several sheets of papers out of his briefcase. "You sign it, we zip back in time, you get the girl, and live happily ever after."

My eyes narrowed, and my lips pressed together so tight they hurt, and my eyes shot daggers as I glared at him. But he was too high pressure of a salesman to realize I was tired of hearing him talk. My irritation evident in my voice, it was all I could do to keep from yelling. "And just what do you get out of the deal, my life savings?"

Satan clasped his hands where his heart should have been,

and with a big- toothy, smile, laughed sounding like a con man sucking in a mark, he said. "You strike me to the quick, Sir. Actually, I gain no financial reward by providing you with the opportunity to achieve your heart's desire. My contract simply states that in the event of your death, I collect your soul."

It was my turn to grab my heart and laugh. "All you want is my soul, so what happens, you take me back to my college days, me and cheating bitch hook up, marry, and you kill me…she gets the insurance, you get my soul and I'm stuck in hell for the rest of eternity?"

The Devil cocked an eyebrow, his voice suddenly soft as though telling me a great secret. "Not at all, Bob, you will be young once again, you and the 'cheat' will hook up, get married, you live a full life and then I take you to hell for all of eternity when you die." He checked his notebook and smiled. "All in all, not a bad deal. As I remember, she was great in the sack and your favorite comment was something about a golf ball and a garden hose, back then."

Watching Satan grin. In all the books and movies, I had viewed, the sex angle always worked when he was negotiating with a guy for his soul.

I leaned back in my chair. Picking up my tea, I stared out the front window as though in deep thought, perhaps considering the deal. Despite thinking this was a scam, I nodded at memories of Marianne and our adventures.

He slid the papers across the table with a lacquered fountain pen he removed from his breast pocket.

Satan winked at me with a smile of knowing his victory was at hand. "Just like the car commercials, my boy … just sign and drive."

I leaned forward and placed my elbows on the table. I stared at the contract but wasn't reading a word. I was ready to get up and walk out of the diner, but my darker side spoke up. This guy interrupted lunch. It is time you played with him for a bit. Let's waste his time and not close the deal.

"Slow down, Bucko, I haven't made up my mind. That was a long time ago. After all these years I've forgotten what she looked like." I held out my hand. "I'm sure your research team has photos."

"Hmmmm, that's a demand seldom asked when I'm trying to help someone, but I think there may be a few in the file." This time, the Devil extracted a blood-red folder, from his bag of horrors, with my name blazoned across the front in huge gold letters.

Balancing the file on his lap, he opened the folder and removed several sheets of heavy paper and laid them on the table, face up.

One sheet held several small photos of when we first met, others held dating activities, trips, and special occasions the, theater, concerts, and parties. The sequence of papers showed the development of our relationship, falling in heat and later love.

The next few had several photos of private activities, including full frontal nude photos of Marianne, her favorite positions, and other demonstrations of her talents in and out of bed. The last sheet showed me in various states of depression and loss when she walked out.

My mind reeled. I had forgotten how beautiful and talented she was in those days. She had the unquenchable desire for positions and exotic locations for romantic activities.

"Ah, she was a beautiful girl, and loved entertaining me, and apparently Dennis, and who knows how many others." I thrust the pictures at the devil. "Now convince me … Why should I be interested in her now? Show me photos of the past twenty plus years."

The Devil let out a sigh. His shoulders slumped and he shook his head. "You are a man questioning a proposal of happiness, Bob. Look at this beautiful woman, this is who you would be returning too … hot, sexy, man-pleaser … What are you waiting for? Sign the contract and she is all yours."

Crossing my arms, I said, "Photos for the past twenty years, please."

Again, the Devil shook his head and removed a stack of photos from his case. "You have to realize, Bob, this is her current lifeline. When you sign with me, all that changes, plus you will be happy the rest of your life."

I stared straight into his eyes. I wasn't giving an inch until I examined the current Marianne. I'm not giving in after I see the pictures, either.

Satan placed the photos one by one on the table between them.

I recognized the first picture, engagement announcement to Dennis. The years passed into review, one by one. The love of his life held a baby, then a baby with a toddler. More children arrived in various photos as years progressed.

My jaw fell open, I snapped it shut, "She has seven kids. That's like a new kid every three years or so. She majored in biological science…why didn't she use birth control."

"Dennis wanted a son. They kept trying." Satan answered. "Number eight is due in September, another girl, but they don't know it yet."

The Devil kept dropping photos on the table every fifteen seconds.

I watched a young, vibrant woman change into a tired, worn out shell. Her body was destroyed by a house full of kids.

And Dennis. Oh Dennis … what a change … no longer the football star. In one of the last family pictures, he had a beer in his hand and the gut to match. He needed a shave, a haircut, and some new clothes without holes or patches, perhaps cleaned and pressed.

"So Robert, are you ready to sign the contract and save her from a life of diapers, screaming children, and rescue her from Dennis?" Once again, he offered me the fountain pen. "All I need is your signature, right where the 'X' is printed at the bottom of the page."

I ignored the pen and picked up the contract to read the entire document. It was very straight forward. I would travel to the past, be young again, and marry the girl of my dreams. In return I would forfeit my soul at the time of expiration. All for the opportunity to spend my life with Marianne.

There was no guarantee of life span, happiness, or anything except the opportunity to collect the woman of my youth.

Satan shoved the fountain pen under my nose. "Just prick your finger with the point and sign, Robert. You will have happiness for as long as you live."

His conquering smile drooped as I took the pen and set it on the table next to the contract. I picked up the photos and studied them once again. He nodded his head at times, smiled, and shook it when I stared at the early photos.

I tossed the photos across the table, picked up the pen and sat it at the bottom of the contract. Rolling the contract into a tube like a scroll, I presented it to Satan as a knight bringing news to a king in olden days.

"You may be the Prince of Darkness and know everyone's hidden desires, wants and needs. Marianne will always have a warm place in my heart. You want my soul … and I don't even know for sure if I have one, but your interest in it makes me stop and consider the possibility of personal ownership. I think I'll pass." I shook my head, "To return to the past only gives me the opportunity to make the same mistakes a second time. I think I will focus on making new mistakes in this time and place. You have a great day."

I stood, placed a tip on the table and walked out the door. I returned to work with a new outlook on life. Deep down, I acknowledged I was happy in my success. But I had missed several opportunities to meet other women as I never stopped longing for the woman in my past. One thing is certain, Marianne was not the woman for me … then, or now.

"Today starts a new life for Mr. Robert Tidwell, new friends and a chance to meet someone looking for a middle-aged man."

When I entered the building, Jennifer, the ever-observant security guard watched everyone as they entered the building. Her eyes seemed to sparkle and her smile genuine as I walked to the desk.

"Jennifer, you look lovely today."

Her face flushed, and her eyes flashed with joy from the compliment. Her smile grew more pleasant as I stood in front of her desk.

"I am going to go out on a limb. This is a true compliment coming from me to you … I like a woman in uniform ... actually, I like you in uniform. Would you consider going out to dinner sometime?"

Jennifer turned beet red. She focused on the counter for a heartbeat, then brought her eyes back to mine. "That sounds lovely, Mr. Tidwell."

"Please, call me Robert or Bob, whichever you prefer. How about tomorrow, after work?"

"As it happens, I don't have any plans for tomorrow."

"Excellent. Where would you like to go?"

Jennifer swiped at the air. "Oh, I'm not that picky. Surprise me." She scribbled something on a sticky note and offered it to him. "Here's my cell number. Give me a call later and we'll work out the details."

I grinned and made a show of putting the note in my wallet before I headed for the elevator. As I stood at the shiny metal doors waiting for the next car, I bounced on the balls of my feet and muttered, "Thanks Devil. You opened my eyes to the beauty around me and not some long-lost memory. And it didn't cost me a soul."

10

UNLIMITED POWER

"WHAT I'M SAYING, Dr. Scott, is this machine will explode before it can generate enough power to provide electricity for the campus, let alone Washington D.C. or the surrounding states. The unit is just too small to distribute that much energy. You'll blow the motor somewhere around 1-billion gigawatts." Yuri screamed. "That explosion will evaporate the entire eastern seaboard.

Dr. Scott scowled at the middle-aged man. "What do you know … you … you collector of trash? I have PhD's in Applied and Theoretical Physics. I created the formula and built this generator. I am certain it will not only power this campus, but also all of D.C. for a thousand years."

Red-faced, Dr. Scott glared at Yuri. This was not a new discussion and he was tired of this argument with a mere trash collector. "All it requires is one gallon of gasoline to initiate the process. Once started, the perpetual motion will generate electricity, thus providing free power for all of D. C., Virginia, and the other surrounding states. In mere months it will power the country as the generator is mass produced and scattered around the country." The sarcasm in his voice was not lost on the janitor.

"Sir, I have more degrees that you in this field. I was the head of the Quantum Electrodynamics Research Division until the most recent Russian revolution. I studied and built generators for the government that are currently in space. I escaped the purge and came here with the hope of helping this country. I know what I am talking about."

Dr. Scott, either not listening or caring about the other man in the room, poured the gas into the reservoir and primed his machine. "Stand there and watch history being made" Scott shouted in triumph. "Unlimited power for eternity from one gallon of gas."

"Power can be given to all the states, throughout the world ... free power to all, and no carbon footprint or fear of radiation contaminating the land." Scott glared at the man collecting trash. "My name will be in the history books." He announced and pushed the "start" button.

The generator sputtered, then picked up a rhythm and increasing speed. Thirty seconds later, Dr. Scott pushed the green button activating the rotors to produce electric current. Various pieces of equipment, including radios, and clocks were suddenly powered by the machine. Lights on the concourse began to glow in the midday sun.

"You see Yuri, the machine is powering the grid much faster than I predicted. The experiment is going swimmingly."

The Russian looked out the window, as the power from the generator overrode the electrical grid on campus, the lights outside the science building burned brighter and brighter, until the weaker bulbs exploded.

The smaller lights running along the sidewalks were next. Bulbs blew like rapid machinegun firing at a charging enemy. As the power continued to grow in force, the larger streetlights didn't fade, they exploded with glass falling on the people below.

Startled as he watched the bulbs shatter and the loud, gun

fire like popping sounds, Yuri looked back at the gauges. The needle on the output gauge continued to swing toward the right at an alarming rate. Below the gauges, the meters registering power used on the grid climbed into the red. "Doctor, you should look. There is a problem."

"For God's sake, Yuri, you just can't stand my experiment succeeding." He said, walking to the machine. "Holy Mother of Power." He exclaimed. Output from the machine had reached 1.8 billion gigawatts, while use was holding steady at .75 million. The entire system glowed from the heat as the generator continued to produce more and more power.

Yuri searched for a switch, a button … anything to shut the generator down, but was unable to locate it.

He looked at the professor, "Well Dr. Scott, congratulations on a successful experiment, however I do have one complaint … you forgot to add an off switch."

11

IT'S THE SUDDEN STOP

Charles Montgomery sauntered towards the deli a block up and a block over from his office. His morning started out bad and plummeted to worse after he got to work. He had been tied up with a client, sat through a meeting his boss should have attended, then he had the nerve to chew him out because he wasn't at his desk.

He bit his tongue so as not to inform his boss that he had attended the three-hour meeting instead of ducking out, he would have been getting work done.

He needed to decompress before he bludgeoned his boss with his own stapler.

His friend and counterpart, Alex Simpson, also attended the meeting so the company would have confirmation of the discussions. As a part of company policy, especially problem customers, a note was placed on the door of the conference room that all meetings would be recorded. Three Gunk people, qualified as a pain in the ass contract. Alex taped the entire three-hour fiasco.

"They may make the best explosives in the world," said Alex after the meeting, "But they need several ounces shoved where the sun don't shine and have the crap blown out of them."

Charles smiled, "And I would help you shove the explosive and light the fuse."

Since Charles had handled most of the meeting, Alex offered to cover for him so he could take an extra hour for lunch. "Get out of the building, sit down and relax." Alex told him.

No need to twist his arm, Charles grabbed his jacket and waved his thanks to Alex as he fast walked to the door.

The meeting replayed in his head and pushed his blood pressure up a notch as he walked. Those three clowns are four-star assholes. It was like working with The Three Stooges. His hands turned into fists with each step, his face turned red, he gritted his teeth to the point that his jaw was beginning to hurt, and his forehead was also breaking out in a sweat caused by the frustration ... They make demands that are impossible to meet. A visit to Gunk Inc. for a meeting would be a lot of fun ... *I could paint three executive suites blood red from ceiling to floor.*

He turned the corner and was blocked by a crowd focused on the building across the street. People spilled over the sidewalk to the barricades that blocked off a large open space from the edge of the sidewalk to the center of the street.

Following the crowd's line of sight, Charles spotted a man standing at the edge of the roof. Something about the man seemed familiar.

As he slowly shoved his way to the barricades, he counted ten windows going up. He calculated at least one- hundred twenty-foot drop, depending on the height of the ceilings and space between floors. If the guy jumped, he would certainly get the job done.

As Charles moved from the center of crowd in towards the corner and end of the barricade, he wondered how much blood would splatter on the ghoulish spectators as they attempted to push themselves closer to the action.

He couldn't make out the man's face as he was too high up. His stomach growled, urging him to move along. This was none of his business, anyway. Besides, he had enough of his own problems.

He worked his way along the wooden horse. If he could make his way to the corner, he could cross at the intersection to the deli. With luck, I can get a seat by the window and enjoy a fresh made sandwich while watching the drama playing out on the street.

He reached the edge of the building and was preparing to jay walk to cross the street when one of the officers leaning against the roadblock and spoke into his radio. "Yes sir, Command just told me he is identified as Robert Faulkner, we're trying to find his wife in the hopes she can help talk him down."

Charles froze, his feet too heavy to lift.

Bob Faulkner was his best friend. Bob and Ellie had been half of the four musketeers for the past nine years. They became friends at the golf course years ago when they were assigned as a foursome. Sara and Ellie became friends before the game was over. Over the years, the four did everything together, dinners, theaters, vacations and the two women shopped together as often as possible. As time passed Sarah and Ellie would say they were unofficial sisters

Charles couldn't let his friend stand on the ledge without knowing what was going on. He tapped the officer on the shoulder. "Sir, I know Bob, he is my best friend. Do you think I could go up and try to talk to him?"

The officer looked at Charles as though he didn't believe him but spoke into his radio. "Captain, this is officer Parks. I have a guy here that says he knows our jumper and they are best friends. He wants to know if he can come up and try to talk him down."

Officer Parks listened to the Captain's through his earpiece. And replied. "No sir, there is still no word on his wife's location. Units have been sent to the home, her office and any other country clubs or organization meetings she may be attending."

Again, Officer Parks listened through his earpiece. Shaking his head, he said. "Okay," Officer Parks pointed toward the front door. "When you enter the building, an officer will escort you down a short hallway, and ride along in the elevator to the top floor. Someone will escort you to the roof. Good luck."

With a brief nod, he was dismissed him and turned his attention back to the ever-growing crowd. "Alright, you vultures, move back."

In less than five minutes, Charles was escorted to a medium sized conference room that held a long table, filled with cops communicating with people in the field, a few extra chairs and three large windows, all open. His escort introduced him to Captain Shaw.

The two men shook hands. "Before I start explaining things, I want to make sure this is your friend." Shaw said while escorting Charles to the center window.

After a long look, Charles answered, "Yes sir, that's Robert Faulkner, my best friend for over nine years."

The pair walked back to the table and sat down. "Charles, I'm the chief negotiator in the event of hostages or jumpers. I can't get through to him." His fingers thumped on the table. "He has been up there two hours, and we can't get him to talk."

Shaw looked down at the table, "I've tried to get him to talk … tell me why he is up here but all he does is mumble and none of what he says makes since. Most of the time he just looks as me but doesn't respond."

Charles followed Shaw's head as it raised and looked out the window. "That's why I agreed to let you come up. The key here is to speak soft, agree with him, no matter how crazy he sounds, and encourage him to get off the ledge and join us on the roof." Shaw nodded his head, "I don't think he will jump, at least for the minute, but," Shaw paused and turned back to Charles, "Whether he falls or jumps, his body would be flattened to a wet, bloody, pulp when he hits the sidewalk. I would appreciate it if you could help me keep that from happening."

Charles stood, "Let's see how he reacts to me."

The two climbed out the window. Shaw leaned against the wall as Charles walked slowly to the ledge. He tried to swallow past the dry patch in the back of his throat, but he didn't have any spit. He was amazed at how calm he sounded when he spoke softly to his friend's back.

"Hey Bob. It's Charlie. Can I come over and talk?"

Bob turned enough to glanced over his shoulder. The dark circles around his eyes and wind-blown hair caught Charles by surprise. His clothing was wrinkled, top two buttons were opened, tie pulled halfway down his shirt.

"Charlie, what are you doing here? How did the cops find you? I'm afraid you can't help me. I've done some terrible things."

"Long story short. I was on my way to lunch and had to get through the crowd below. Heard a cop say your name and identified myself as your friend. The rest is history."

Taking slow careful steps Charles closed the gap between him and his friend. Standing several feet off to the side, he leaned with his arms and elbows on the riser and looked over the ledge.

He gave a long slow whistle. "That's a long drop buddy. How long have you been standing here?"

"Long enough. I can't seem to make myself take the last step."

"Sounds like you want to come back to the roof. I'll give you a hand if you like."

"No. You don't understand Charlie, I am a terrible man who doesn't deserve to live."

"Aren't your legs getting tired?" Charles said trying to change the subject.

Bob nodded, "Yeah, but I've got good balance and I can lean against the wall if I get vertigo."

"Well it sounds like you have a plan to stay up here for days, if not longer." Charles said and smiled at his friend.

"Can I sit on the ledge with you for a while? I won't grab you are anything, but it will sure make it easier to talk to you."

"I don't think that would be wise." He said, "Then the police will have two people on the ledge and that doubles the odds of two people on the sidewalk instead of one."

"I understand," Charles countered, "But there were a lot of stairs to climb getting here. Besides, if I'm beside you, the police won't try anything, they would be afraid of pushing me over with you if they didn't make the grab."

Bob studied his friend and nodded. "Why not. You're the only friend I got. At least for now."

Charles climbed over the riser and slid down to sit as he leaned forward so as not to lose his balance and fall over the edge. Using his arms, he raised himself up a bit and slid closer to his best friend.

Taking a deep breath to help calm his nerves he scooted back against the riser and tried to relax. Looking out toward the crowd he realized they had pushed the barricades farther back and were now in the center of the street. The chant "Jump … Jump" echoed all the way to the roof.

Hands on his knees, Charles leaned over to see if there was any new activity the street. Almost overextending he wobbled forward on the thin ledge. Bob grabbed his friend's sport coat and kept him from falling.

Charles caught his breath before speaking. Pointing across down to the intersection then straight ahead. "Media" … Someone had made it to the roof of the building on the other side street and taking photos. Another television station got the jump on the other local stations and was setting up on the roof with a reporter standing off to the side.

Charles shook his head. This is turning into a three-ring circus.

Sliding to the end of the ledge, Bob gently poked his companion in the ribs. "This is nothing, just wait until they get the rest of the story" His voice sounded sad, matching his comments about being a terrible person.

"Tell me more. I'd like to know what is going on."

Bob stared at the cameras across the street. "No, I want to keep you as my best friend for now. My secret."

Charles glanced at his watch. He had been on the ledge for over an hour.

He turned a bit and caught the attention of Captain Shaw, and beckoned him over. "Sir, I was wondering if you could do two things for me? "He said dropping a business card from his pocket to the roof. "First, would have some one stop by my office and tell my employer why I will be late returning from lunch," He paused allowing Shaw to step back but remain in sight. "Second, could you get a couple of subs and sodas from the deli on the far corner?"

Shaw gave a thumbs up and got on his walkie-talkie.

They talked quietly for several minutes about mundane things like baseball and poker. Bob wouldn't discuss what drove him to this thought of suicide.

As the two men ate, Bob started talking about his work, the pressures he and his wife were experiencing. Charles watched his friend take a deep breath as his eyes began to fill with tears. His voice wavered as he continued to say over and over, "I've done things, terrible things that will hurt people I care for when the story gets out.

"What could you possibly do that would cause your friends to desert you?" Charles asked. "You know you can always count on me for support when times get tough."

Bob looked his friend in the eye and shook his head and once again stared down at the crowd.

Charles decided that whatever his friend had done, it placed him in his own personal hell, and would be forced to live with it, or jump and end it.

Bob's eyes glazed over as he followed the crowd focused on his sitting on the ledge. From time to time the shout of "Jump", Jump" would echo in the streets. People getting off work enlarged the crowd as more men and women continued to congregate in the hope of watching the man fall.

"You know Bob, I've been sitting up here with you for hours. You keep repeating you did something terrible. I'm beginning to think you just want attention." Charles said. "So, tell me, just what evil things you have done to disappoint the entire world, your wife and your co-workers, and our friendship that would force you up on this roof? Tell me now or I am going home to my wife and leave you here to rot."

Bob stood on the ledge to stretch his legs. He looked over at this friend, "I have betrayed you, your wife, my wife and myself." He sobbed. "I told Ellie I wanted a divorce this morning. I've had enough of her and all the crap she loves to dish out when we are alone."

"Oh man, you two are such a great couple. Why would you want to get a divorce, lose everything you have built during your fifteen years of marriage?"

"Oh Charlie, the only way I can explain this is to be blunt and it is going to really hurt you." Bob said.

Taking a deep breath, he began his confession. "For the past year, I've been having an affair with Kathy." He stared down at his friend, his eyes showing the shame he felt in telling this secret. "I'm so sorry. I know she's your wife and we're best friends, but we were drawn to each other. She fills needs Ellie won't even discuss."

Charles remained calm as he listened to his friend. "So, you and Kathy planned to run off together?"

"Well, that was my plan when I walked out of the house and called Kathy. I could still hear Ellie screaming in the background. I thought it would be better if I let her know that Ellie would be on the warpath. That's when everything really went to hell."

Charles continued to watch his friend. "How did you think Ellie would react to your plan Bob? Did you think she would wish you the best and move out?" He said in disbelief.

"I don't know, man. But I didn't know she would go into such a tirade." He shook his head and continued. "Other neighbors leaving for work could hear what she was saying."

Bob shook his arms and dropped them in frustration, "Anyway, I called Kathy, told her what I did and told her to pack a bag, we were leaving town. I cleaned out the bank account and the safety deposit box the day before. I told her we could leave and start a new life."

Charles glared at the other man. "Just what was my wife's response?"

Bob was unable meet to his gaze. Tears streamed down his cheeks. "She told me I was crazy. It was all just fun and games and we had no relationship. She laughed when she said I wasn't the first and wouldn't be the last."

Taking deep breaths to calm down, his voice became a whisper. "But that's not the worst of it." He paused. His lower lip quivered, as he stared down at his friend, "Between Ellie yelling and Kathy laughing at me … I snapped"

Charles noted Bob's toes extended off the concrete ledge. *I wonder if he is building the courage to jump.*

"Oh Charlie, I went back in the house. I thought I could reason with her, and we could work things out. She screamed and screamed, calling me the most horrid names. I just couldn't take it. I grabbed the plaster gargoyle from the end table and hit her in the head. Over and over and over. Hell, I kept hitting her until she had no head, I killed her." Bob put his back to the wall. Hands raised, he focused on the crowd on the street. The spectator's chants grew in intensity. "JUMP! JUMP!"

"Damn, Bro." Charlie said, as he began kicking his legs, acting as though they were cramping. "I guess you did step way over the line. I don't mean to add to your troubles." He said turning and using one hand to hold onto the wall, he safely began to kneel in an attempt to stand. "I was home when you called this morning."

His grin took on a cold, calculated expression. "I was standing at the kitchen door and heard her end of the conversation. After the two of you hung up, Kathy confessed and told me what you offered."

Charlie remained stationary as his expression turned emotionless. "I forgave her for all her indiscretions. I even forgive you." He said in a monotone that was loud enough to be heard by the various officers standing close by. "You, however, are between a rock and a hard place. You killed your wife, and if you snapped, what vengeance did you take out on my wife for rejecting you?"

He placed an arm on the riser and prepared to stand. "You might as well jump since this is a death penalty state. Either way, you are a dead man."

Charles continued to look his friend in the eyes. In a near whisper, he confessed. "You are set up my friend. You see, I forgave Kathy by killing her, and with your confession about killing your wife, and my response about what vengeance would you take on Kathy … You are now a double murderer."

Head bowed, Charles began to bring his back knee up to stand, while his front foot kicked the back of Bob's ankle. The

Achilles ankle gave way and his body fell forward off the ledge.

"Bob don't." Charlie shouted and his friend plunged to the ground below, hitting several by-standers before splattering on the asphalt.

A police officer rushed forward and grabbed Charles' arm before he was over balanced and joined his friend below. After being helped to the roof, Charles turned to see the body lying in the middle of the street. Shaking his head, "I guess he thought he could just fly away from his problems."

One of the officers commented, "That was a hell of a fall."

Charles smiled. "It wasn't the fall that put him out of his misery." He walked toward the room. "It was the sudden stop."

12

THE CHALLENGE

I SHOULD HAVE KNOWN BETTER. I remember all the Predator movies, especially the one where the humans are taken to a planet and hunted by aliens. But I was hard up for money and taking on a gladiator challenge didn't seem that difficult. After all, I was proficient in various forms of martial arts, using a variety of lethal ancient and modern weapons, plus ten years as a navy seal, and keeping up with my skills, I would have a better than average chance for the One-Hundred-thousand-dollar check.

I figured this would be a walk in the park. Work through an obstacle course, fire at targets for points. They might even have dummies to attack and acquire points on time, following the course, and hitting targets. There was no limit on the types of weapons or skills.

All applications were accepted, but only twenty contestants would be selected. Everyone would meet the day before the challenge and could form teams, or a contestant could remain independent. The team or an individual surviving the tournament would win.

It took six weeks before receiving a reply. A priority envelope arrived at my apartment containing an acceptance letter, passport, and airplane ticket. I had two weeks to make any necessary arrangements, organize, and leave town.

Assuming I would be selected, I thought ahead … I had my financial affairs in order before the letter arrived, as well as intensifying my training. The day after receiving the letter, I requested four weeks' vacation from work and gave my boss a sealed envelope to be opened if I failed to return.

"Look, Bob, I'm not quitting." I said as he looked at the envelope, "I'm going on an adventure, a survival exercise. I may need the extra time off to recover and rest up from the competition."

I leaned forward in my chair and put my arms on his desk. "I still have more vacation time remaining. If you can extend my time out, great, but if you have to let me go, I understand."

Bob slid the envelop into his center drawer. "Don't get killed and be careful." He said, "But knowing you, I'll be happy if you just stay alive and return."

I nodded and stood.

"By the way," Bob said, "finish up everything today … your vacation starts tomorrow. I will divide up all your work so when you return you won't be behind."

We shook hands. "Good luck."

Dismissed, I returned to my desk and began wrapping up my ongoing projects.

That evening I reviewed my list of all the clothing and equipment I needed and began setting everything I had on hand on the living room floor. My purchase list was rather long, but I had contacts that would eliminate wait times for certain weapons.

With extra time off, I was up before the sun and working out in my twenty-four-hour gym for a couple hours each morning, stretching then lifting heavy weights and increase my stamina with a variety of cardio exercises. Mid-day, I was at one of my dojo's training full contact with a private instructor. After lunch, another dojo with weapons training. The rest of the afternoon was getting in touch with my special contacts and acquiring my other equipment needs. Evenings I trained in a private dojo that had no name on the door and required a special degree of skill to be invited.

I contacted a former seal buddy and joined in some survival training classes and exercises. Three days of Urban and Three days of Jungle Survival.

With one last review of my equipment, I packed each item as needed, that evening. I stowed the bags by the door.

I spent Sunday stretching and relaxing awaiting my ride. A limo arrived in the early evening. Traffic was light, we entered the secured gate at the airport in about an hour and stopped at a private hanger, everything was unloaded and stowed in the belly of a twin turbo aircraft. The plane was in the air within minutes.

THE PLANE DESCENDED after several hours of flying. A Canadian flapped in the breeze on top of the airport flagpole. We taxied to another aircraft sitting on the tarmac.

Exiting the plane, a table was set up at the foot of the stairs. My passport was stamped twice, the first for Canada, the second for China. I was sent on my way. I followed my baggage being pulled on a cart to a second aircraft. My equipment was once again stored. I started up the steps and realized the windows were covered. I stepped inside. The seats faced backwards, there were four other people seated in the plane. Muscle was everywhere.

I made my way to the only seat available, close to the cockpit. To look tough, I squinted my eyes and swaggered just a bit as I passed each person.

Two bulked men with that blank, thousand-yard stare kept their eyes on me as I passed. There were two athletically built women who could pass for men in any gym. They wore their tight butt shorts and wife beater tee shirts to display muscles on top of muscles. One woman twisted her neck so I could hear the bones pop as I walked by. Their eyes were as cold as steel. The brunette ran her thumb across her throat as I passed by.

Truth be told, I felt like a deer on opening season. What have I gotten myself into?

Engines started and we began to taxi. How did the pilots know I was ready? After attaching my seat belt, I turned and scanned the wall above the cockpit door. I spotted the rounded dark glass indicating a security camera.

The door between the passengers and the flight crew remained closed. There was no way to see what direction the aircraft headed, adding a variety of banks and turns, the only thing I could determine was that we flew long enough for me to take a nap.

I awoke with the squeal of tires as the plane landed. No one got out of their seats to stretch. I realized we were taking on fuel when I heard talking and the pumping of the gas truck outside the window. Soon, we were air borne once again.

I awoke from another long nap with the plane bouncing on unleveled ground. I checked my watch and realized that this leg of the trip had lasted over six hours.

The passenger door opened, and a metal ladder leaned up against the body of the plane. The pilot stepped out of the cockpit. His face looked as though it were carved in granite. As he walked to the back of the aircraft. He didn't smile or remove his sunglasses. "Your baggage will be on the truck. Get out and don't tip the ladder. If you fall and break something, well, that will be your tough luck."

Glancing down the aisle as the men stood to exit, he continued, "Once you disembark, you may relieve yourselves in the bushes … You aren't staying at a fancy resort so don't be shy, get used to it. There is a van waiting and you will be provided with a boxed lunch. Good luck to all of you."

As I stepped off the ladder and headed for the tall grass, the other four had spaced themselves out. There was no shyness, the woman simply dropped their pants, turned and faced plane. Relieved, we all headed for our transportation.

Our 'van' was a short yellow bus with one row of single seats. The lunch consisted of two bottles of warm water, a stale sandwich, and a cookie. If this is what they feed us, I'm glad I brought MRE's with me.

We rode through desert. There was no road, just sand and a few scrub trees scattered here and there. After an hour, we entered the bush. There were trees, vines and a variety of plants that went from sparse smatterings to view blocking, unkempt, they were growing wild and free.

Two hours later, we turned off the dirt road onto a winding path which ended at a series of wooden huts. I had seen villages in third world nations that had more to offer. At one end of the line of small wooden buildings was a larger structure. Off to the side, there were picnic tables sitting outside. Behind the tables were cauldrons over an open fire, a couple of old grills sat off to the side using the cut sides of fifty-five-gallon drums.

Next to the 'cook house' stood a larger building with open double doors and a few windows. It was too dark to see inside, but presumably it was the meeting room where we would be briefed on the event.

Spaced at an angle, beyond the meeting room, were wooden shanties. Ah, home sweet home. Large enough to fit four people, but it would be tight quarters.

A man stepped out of the dark building wearing desert camo. "What are you waiting for, a special invitation? Get off the bus and stand on the line in front of me." He commanded.

The lines were short and staggered so he could observe us

individually. I took a position on the last line. I assumed first on the plane first in line.

Five men carried our bags and stood beside our leader. "Raise your hand when your gear is next to me. Come and get it and place it to your right."

After we had our bags beside us, he issued another command. "All right 'Fresh Meat' open your equipment bags and lay everything out on the ground for inspection."

We aligned our gear, smallest items to largest. My jaw dropped as I examined the various high-powered weapons. I was amazed that there were three AR15's, an M-1 Sniper rifle. I also counted at least four pistols per person, knives, swords, and a variety of other silent weapons.

I carried a bolt action rifle and a couple of HK 9mm weapons. Mine were lethal, but nothing that could separate a man from his soul and spirit from a thousand yards. Well, Harold, you've always been an overachiever, now is the time to put out 200 percent.

"Alright, get in the meeting room. Spread out, no talking. There are cold drinks and snacks available. The latrine is behind the building, in the brush. The second group will be here within the hour." He shouted, "And remember, I will shoot anyone talking to another contestant."

We headed toward the open doors as five workers walked out with bags of flour to create new lines for the next arrivals.

The meeting room held a podium at the front, a large faced clock hung above it, and ten small desks with chairs spaced in a semi-circle around the room. The bare plywood walls were discolored from years of use.

I adjusted my watch making sure it was synchronized with the clock. I noticed all the others doing the same.

I heard the bus arrive. The Commander gave the same orders to the additional contestants.

After a half hour, three women and two men entered the

room. Each glared at the rest of us as they picked up cold drinks and a quick bite to eat.

"Listen up people," the Commander barked as he stepped through the door. "First, there were supposed to be twice as many of you in this contest, but the other selectees didn't qualify or in some instances, chickened out. It is just the ten of you. It changes the dynamics but not the outcome. This is now a three-day challenge. You will have one hour to meet and talk among yourselves. By nightfall, if any of you wish to team up, do so. The sooner you decide the longer you have to coordinate your plans. Teams may stay in the same cottage, no more than two members to a team. Individuals sleep alone. Keep in mind that if your team wins, and a member decides to go rogue on their partner, the survivor will not have to split the money."

He looked around the room, "A team can survive or an individual, but not both." His smile was cold as he continued, "to quote an old movie series … There can be only one."

Hands clasped behind his back, he paraded around the room, his eyes bright with excitement. "To be perfectly clear, this is a Gladiator / Survivor challenge. If you lose … you die."

I hid my short gasp, looking at the other people, A couple of people smiled and licked their lips while the others had no reaction to the announcement. I pulled out all my correspondence from my shirt pocket. There weren't that many pages, just the contract and list of contacts in the event of an injury. There was no mention of survival of the fittest, but now that I knew the rules. I grasped the meanings in the wording of the invitation and release forms.

"I need everyone to turn to the very back page of your contract packet. This is a final release form which gives us permission to return your body to family, or friends or another organization for burial."

The other nine people immediately flipped open the

packet, filled in the blanks and signed the form. I hesitated for a second, then did the same. There was no getting out of this.

"You are dismissed. Everyone can finalize their decisions on teams and present them to me at the evening meal. After that, I will review the rules before lights out." He left without saying another word.

I made my way over to the men and was disregarded. My guess … I don't look like a survivable partner. Some looked at me like I would be their first victim and easiest target, others as if I were a joke. Okay, so much for team sportsmanship.

The women kept to themselves.

Since I wasn't going to get anywhere with the others, I went out and collected my things. Everything sat next to the building, guarded by the same men. They watched as I picked up my equipment and headed toward the huts.

I selected the first cabin. It was simple living, two bunk beds placed across the room from the other, a small nightstand. There was no bedding on the thin mattress. Home sweet home. The advantage of being a single contestant was I could lay everything out on the bottom bunk of the extra bed.

I organized my survival essentials, food – water – first aid and the like, then packed them for easy carrying. From the top bunk I organized my weapons and began cleaning guns and sharpening knives.

When the dinner bell rang, I made my way to the dining hall while the other nine stood by their equipment, yelling at each other.

Not my circus, not my monkeys.

I went up to the serving line and collected my meal. The food looked delicious and the smell made my mouth water. My tray filled, I sat down at the nearest table and dug into my food.

One of the men, big and hairy with a forehead like a Neanderthal, barreled up to my table. With an ape like snarl,

"What did you do with our shit?" He shouted, as the remainder of the group moved up behind him.

"What are you talking about? I didn't touch any of your gear. Why would I … especially with the four guys watching every move made outside the big building?"

The Neanderthal looked around and spotted the four-armed men who had covered our equipment. He headed towards them, ready to tear them apart.

"If I were you, I would get my meal before they close up shop or the guards shoot you on an empty stomach. Our Leader will be here, you can ask him what happened." I said and returned to my hot supper.

One of the women spoke up, "Why don't we just search your cabin?"

I smiled at her, "Nice to meet you too. I wouldn't advise it. If you tried, I would stop you. I don't want my equipment broken. Also, if you are lucky and get passed me, be aware that I had time to set a couple traps. You may take me out, but no points, since the game hasn't started yet, and with your injuries, you won't win either."

I took a bite of my food and looked up at the group, a stupid smile plastered on my face. I think it confused them, since they mumbled to each other as they made their way to go their meal. They sat as far away from me as they could. I wondered if my bluff gave them second thoughts about my ability to kill them all.

They had divided into obvious teams and sat as separate units at the various tables. Two men and one woman in a group, AKA Neanderthal, Broken Nose, and Muscle woman, two women, "Barbie and Black Widow, in a second, a man and woman teamed up, "Beast" and "Beauty", each team sat with an empty table between them. That left one woman, "Steel Eyes", another man, Hulk, and me fighting as individuals.

"Ladies and gentlemen," the leader's voice boomed, "I

see you have selected your teams. Very good. Some of you have forgotten teams consist of two individuals, not three. Whoever leaves this threesome may fight alone or choose one of the other three people as a teammate," he said as he looked at a particular table.

He looked over the group. "Ah, some of you noticed and were quite vocal about the results of your equipment inspection." His voice echoed off the walls. "I heard your accusations. You should all know, my men went through your baggage."

Hulk and Broken nose stood, knocked, their chairs to the floor as they started toward the front of the room. Two guards trained rifles on the men in a flash.

"Sit down," he commanded pointing to the two men.

"I am Leroy Ringer. I run this camp and the contest. You may call me 'Sir' when we speak. Your equipment was inspected by my men. All explosives were removed. You have your rifles and pistols, however, you only have one-hundred rounds of ammunition for each weapon. If you aren't a good shot, get close. All knives, daggers, garrotes, and the like remain in your bags as does any food. Canteens may be filled at any time from the barrels at the edge of the serving line.

"As for the rules, this contest runs for three days. At the end, anyone surviving must make their way back to this spot no later than noon the fourth day. If you feel as though you are the only survivor, arrive on the third. Someone will be waiting for your return. If more than one person has survived that is not a team member, there will be hand to hand combat until one person remains. Any questions?"

One of the women asked, "When do we start and where is the playing field?"

"The game starts tomorrow, you pick the time." He scanned the warriors with a look that let you think he knew a secret, "the field starts 100 yards in any direction from this compound. There is yellow tape indicating the boundaries."

He looked at me, "When you finish eating, we will inspect your weapons."

I nodded, knowing the guards would let him know when I returned to my 'cottage'. Since I wasn't involved in the team selection process, I jumped the gun in collecting my gear.

"If there are no other questions, Breakfast will be served at five in the morning for those still here. Rest well." He completed an about-face and walked away.

Everyone was spaced out enough that quiet conversation couldn't be heard. Steel Eyes walked up to me and gave me the once over.

"You don't look like a killer or an assassin, why are you here?" she asked, "I wanted a teammate, but you don't look strong enough and the other guy is just too nasty for my tastes."

I shrugged, "I miss-read the invitation, applied and was accepted. I have a few skills, but going up against sniper rifles and pistols, I'll have to really be on my game."

She sat beside me, "Cheryl," she said, "Level 4 assassin for the Mossad. I don't know about the others. Look, I don't want to team up, but if you see me and watch my back, I'll do the same for you."

"Not a problem. I have no history of killing anyone, but I have taken a lot of survival classes and I think I'm in good shape. I think I can last the three days, and can limit my kills to one."

I gave this young woman a closer look. No more than five-foot-tall, she was athletic had and 'the stare' as well as a blank face. Pretty, but my bet was she kept most men away with her cold attitude. "All right, I won't put myself between you and a bullet, but if I can help, I will."

She touched my hand, "Thanks, same to you."

The sun was beginning to set, she stood, leaning down she whispered, "If you get lonely…you know where I am." Turning she walked to her cabin.

The 'magnificent eight' gathered their equipment and headed to the various huts. The teams bunked together. I wondered who would get laid tonight. The tension was high for all of us and sex is a great reliever of tension.

My equipment inspected, I was left alone with my thoughts for survival during the next three days.

I woke at 11:30, thanks to the vibration of the alarm on my watch. In thirty minutes, the challenge would begin. My plan was to get a head start of the killer professionals by going under the yellow tape at midnight and stay hidden until the end. Let the others kill off as many as they could. Then I'll sweep up the rest. Easy. I scoffed at myself. Yeah, right.

I dressed in the dark before slipping out to the water barrels to fill my canteens. When the clock in the conference room chimed a quiet twelve times. I re-entered my hut leaving the door open as I strapped on my gear.

In less than fifteen minutes, I had everything attached to or on my survival pack and headed for the combat arena. I crawled out and along the side of the hut. I was sneaking out. I didn't want to be seen or heard by any other contestant. In minutes I found the yellow boundary tape.

I crawled several yards from the encampment before standing. Unless someone had come out before midnight, I should be safe … If I was wrong, I would be the first casualty in this contest.

I had no map and we had not been permitted to leave the compound before the games. But from looking over the area yesterday, the best I could do was second guess the terrain until after day light. I had spotted some high ground, not knowing the lay of the land, I traveled terribly slow, feeling my way in the dark. I found a trail thanks to the moon light but followed it while I stayed buried in the brush. My plan was to make better time with the beginning light of day and hoped that there might be a few small caves for protection and shelter.

I used all my stealth techniques to leave as little a trail as possible. I was up against nine pros, come dawn, my head start wouldn't mean shit.

What am I doing? Who do I think I am fooling … they were probably waiting at the tape when the clock struck twelve, or perhaps already in the field, and I was the late comer to join in the contest. I looked around but spotted no movement. Plus, I am still breathing. I just have to be careful.

The sun peeked over the mountains when the sounds of people in the compound echoed up the hills. There were very few voices, and it wasn't time for breakfast. It sounded like staff preparing to cook meals and continue their everyday lives in the compound. However, a few gladiators arrived and started yelling at the cooks, wanting their breakfast.

"Looks like I'm not the only one getting a head start, but I didn't wait for breakfast. If you have food for the field, you can skip breakfast and get into position to eliminate the competition." I said to myself. "I guess some people just don't think ahead."

The thought was sobering. Once again, I broke out in a sweat wondering if I was in the cross hairs of a sniper rifle.

A few of my fellow competitors slept in. I drooled at the smell of hot food as four more gladiators grabbing half cooked eggs and floppy bacon before walking toward the yellow tape. They entered from different spots of the competition area. No one wanted to be a willing target.

As far as I could tell, I may have been the first person to be in a position to snipe one or two before I had to move again. I had Hulk in my cross hairs, when a raucous emanated from the camp. I trained my binoculars on the compound.

Barbie and Black Widow walked up to the cooks. That made five in the field three unaccounted for and these two remaining in camp. The brunette stood stiffly with her arms crossed while the Barbie barked at her. Black Widow shook her head, picked up her pack and stomped off, disappearing into the brush.

Still yelling, Barbie threw her hands in the air screaming, "But I'm starving," she grabbed her gear and followed.

Neither considered the possibility that the eight other members of this competition could be hidden in the competition zone, while watching their tantrums. They certainly made themselves easy targets.

I tracked the two as Barbie stepped up to the yellow tape and looked for her partner. Black Widow was already hidden in the brush, unseen. After ducking under the tape, Barbie took four steps and fell forward grabbing her stomach.

I could see an extra pair of arms driving a bayonet just under the ribs. Black Widow rose to her knees and twisted the blade before pulling the weapon out and slicing the blade across Barbie's throat. The former dropped to the ground. Black Widow showed no remorse over the loss of her partner. She crouched, turned, and continued into the forest.

"One down, eight to go." I said to myself as I scanned other areas of the kill zone. Hulk was nowhere to be found, but I spotted the illegal threesome … Muscle Woman, Broken Nose had teamed up with Neanderthal after crossing into the battle zone. Somewhere during the next few days, one or two of them would probably be killed by their partners. There was no sign of 'I got your back, you got mine' or Beauty and the Beast.

Realizing my camos would not completely protect me from being seen, I cut several pieces of the vegetation and attached it to my hat, arms, and body. It wasn't a Ghillie Suit, but the additional Camouflage might give me an edge, especially with the two snipers in the group.

There was an explosion of a large bore weapon and two smaller bore gunshots echoed off the hills. I dropped to the ground, grabbed my binoculars, and scanned in the area that I thought was the source. Neanderthal raised his sniper rifle to his shoulder to fire a second shot when he suddenly jerked forward as a smaller weapon fired a half breath before his. The bullet caught him in the back of the head.

The next thing I saw, Beast rushed out from the trees to the left and helped his partner, Beauty up and, away from the kill zone. Her arm over his shoulder, she screamed as they blazed a wide trail moving through the edge of the brush for all to see as they made their way up to the rise.

I grabbed my rifle, hoping I could put a bullet in Beast, I might even get two for the price of one. Before I could get a clear shot, the pair reached the top of the rise, he dropped Beauty in the grass and slid away.

I couldn't tell if she were alive or dead. I didn't know if he chose not to waste his energy trying to save her, or realized her blood would leave a trail making him a target, or if he was setting a trap to kill whoever stopped to check on her. I decided to stay put for a few minutes and see what might happen.

Scattered throughout the trees and weeds, I spotted a few of the remaining gladiators making their way toward my hiding place. Lucky for me, they were spread out and were a hundred yards or more from each other.

I climbed, staying low and in the brush as much as possible. My eyes and head kept moving, looking for one of the killers closing in on me while I searched for a cave or something deep in the shadows that would allow me to form a base of operations. I found my hidey hole by accident. I almost missed the small cave. Lucky for me a breeze moved the vines hanging in front of the opening. I noticed the darkness beyond the vegetation.

I wondered if there were other residents inside but decided to take a chance. I'd get out as fast as possible if something crawled, slithered or walked on four legs towards me.

The cave was free of company. I sat inside the mouth of

the cave, keeping an eye on the progress of the competitors. With my binoculars, I could see movement down the hill as I sat just inside the vines. I had a good view but was out of sight of those I considered my enemies. and scanned the area hoping no one had seen me make my way here.

The haven was cool thanks to the brush. The late afternoon sun hid the opening in the deep shadow of the hill. Daylight gave way to dusk. With the opening facing a south east direction, I relaxed a bit as I continued to scan the area below for anyone approaching my position All was clear nearby, so I expanded my search area from left to right.

I found the threesome settling down for the night, Beast, Hulk, and Black Widow had apparently joined forces.

I spotted 'Broken Nose' by accident when he stood making him an easy target for the others. He dropped his gear. Staring at the ground, he undid his belt and dropped his pants. His hairy, bare ass faced me as he bent over and took a what I assumed was a second swing at something.

I grabbed my bow and slid out of my hiding place. Everyone was accounted for except Cheryl. As I crawled closer, I heard him cussing and threatening someone on the ground. "Bitch, if I have to beat you within an inch of your life, I will. Then I will pound you like a two-bit whore in China. When I am finished, I will break bones you never knew you had." He grunted and took another swing at his prisoner. "Keep this up and there won't be enough teeth or anything else to identify you."

He grabbed a leg and tried to flip her onto her stomach. Instead he gasped and fell forward. My guess … a foot caught him somewhere tender.

He straightened and laughed as he slapped her again and again. "You can't stop me you little tiger. I'm going to roll you over and will laugh while you scream."

This time, I saw a boot come up from the ground and kick

him square in the stomach. If she could fight him for just a couple minutes, I would be in range.

"You're mine to have and grind into a puddle." He laughed as he leaned over and punched her with his fist.

I slid down the hill about thirty feet behind him. I was amazed, she kept responding to him. She would kick and say things just to piss him off. She was keeping him off balance.

Despite the attacks, she remained conscious, and threating. Her voice was cold and calculated, but loud enough to let anyone in the vicinity know how to find them. She was a professional. If she died at his hands, she would see to it that he joined her.

"Come on, ass hole, get careless and I'll kick your balls up to your mouth." I heard her say as though she was ordering a slice of pizza from a to-go place on the corner.

I assumed the others could hear the commotion, but it would be a hard climb for anyone to reach the pair. If they even bothered.

I heard his cussing and the sounds of slaps as he hit her again, plus the grunts when she struck back. She was doing her best to fight him off. She wasn't only fighting off his attempt to rape her, but her goal would ultimately be to kill him. It was her nature as an assassin. If he made one mistake, it would be his last. She was 'Walking Death', fully trained and motivated.

I was close enough to know exactly where they were. She most have crawled backward to get out of his reach because he stood, right hand raised to strike as he stepped forward and kicked his leg at her.

Arrow notched, I knelt, aimed, and let fly. It caught him just to the left of his right shoulder. The shaft protruded between his shoulder blade and spine.

Based on the amount of fiberglass showing out of his back, the arrow all but went through him. Broken Nose bellowed and jerked straight up, gun in hand he turned.

Standing, I notched and sent a second arrow. He ducked. I had aimed for his gut. The arrow pierced him through the neck. He dropped like a rock.

I hurried over to retrieve my arrows, and the big man's pack. Cheryl sat on the ground, stunned. Her legs were trapped under his body. A nasty bruise formed on her temple and jaw.

I rolled the body off her legs. "I've got your back. Come with me but stay down. The 'fabulous five' are out there somewhere, probably climbing to our position."

She looked up and appeared to recognize me. I grabbed her backpack, rifle and with my help, she gained her footing. We crouched, using the grass for cover, as we stumbled up the hill. I glanced over my shoulder and spotted, the three of our hunters spread out several hundred yards below. They were about a quarter way up the hill, taking their time. One of them was bound to find Broken Nose just off the path. Fortunately, they were staggered yards apart. Not knowing where anyone else was located. From my view, team, or no team, it was every man for himself.

As we continued to climb, Cheryl regained some her balance and strength. We moved in a zig-zag pattern, up and down the hill. She followed behind me to walk in my footsteps, reducing the trail to a single person. Climbing higher, the dirt gave way to rock. We left no trail to follow. It would appear to the hunters that we simply disappeared.

We circled away and up from my hideout for a half hour and worked our way around boulders. We were out of sight from the other gladiators. She began climbing beside me, once in a while looking over at me with a small smile.

We backtracked to the side of the hill and climbed the rockface. We were scrapped up a bit, but neither of us bleeding. Our soft-soled, jungle boots left no scuff marks. Our camouflaged clothing, enhanced with the twigs and brush, plus plenty of dust from the bare dirt and rocks, allowed us to become a part of the mountain.

We arrived at the cave just as the sun dipped behind the western side of the mountain. We skimmed our way along the outside wall and slipped through the brush concealed entrance. I guided Cheryl to my pallet against the far wall and helped her sit on the bed roll. I leaned her against the wall. After she was settled, I returned to the entrance and scanned the area with my field glasses.

"I don't see any movement, but that doesn't mean much." I said to Cheryl, "They could be out of my field of vision thanks to the cave opening. I lost sight of everybody. The other hunters could be anywhere."

I looked over at her. Eyes closed, breathing regular, she was probably sleeping, but keeping her informed seemed to be the right thing to do.

"Hope they are searching in the wrong direction. They were spread out but following the same line of travel." I continued. "If I could spot one of them, I would have an idea of their location."

Cheryl nodded as though she heard me. I took a break from keeping watch to check on her. She was leaning sideways on the wall and half dozing. I sat her up and moved her body to the corner of the wall. Opening my sterno to heat water and prepare a meal of freeze-dried chicken gunk. "I'm making us a hot meal, so we keep our strength up."

I timed myself by counting from one to one hundred as I scanned outside our cave, then rotate and check on the cooking but only counting to twenty-five.

I scanned the area below one last time before serving our simple meal. Not a sign of the other contestants or movement in the grass.

"I have to give the other warriors credit" I said to Cheryl. "They can stay quiet, and there's been no gunfire in hours."

I served up both meals. "I am more on edge because I

have no idea where they are hiding. For all I know they could be making their way to the fortress. I can only hope that if this is happening, they kill each other."

It was a happy thought, them silently killing each other with Cheryl and I finding their blood-crusted, rotting corpses in the morning. One can only dream.

Dinner was served. "I'm not hungry." She muttered after taking a couple bites, she handed the food back to me. "I just hurt and need to rest."

A large black bruise blossomed over her left eye, and a second one shadowed her right eye. It looked like the two would join across her forehead during the night. I hoped she didn't have a concussion, her skills just might be needed if we were to survive.

Cheryl settled on my blanket and immediately fell asleep. She didn't move and her back was to me, I could see her shoulders raise and lower as she breathed.

NIGHT ARRIVED, I smelled smoke. Armed with my hunting knife, I crawled out past the brush. Using my binoculars, I spotted glow and at times flames of a campfire about a mile or so down and off to the left. There were two silhouettes warming themselves. From the smell coming up the mountain, they had something cooking over the fire.

The silhouettes disappeared. The smell of food evaporated as the fire dimmed. I couldn't tell who was enjoying the warmth and eating. It was careless to let everyone in the field know where they were camping unless they were setting up a trap in the hope of eliminating several contestants at one time.

I slid back inside the cave. I covered my flashlight with a red lens. I could see, but with the brush and the red light, it wouldn't attract attention. I went over and checked on my guest. Her breathing was regular, and she appeared to sleep, thankfully without snoring.

I returned to my guard post. Bow ready and my rifle beside me. If anyone attempted to approach our cave or move the brush away from the entrance, I was ready for the first couple. I removed the hunting knife from my boot, and placed it under my belt, where it would be more readily available if needed. The crickets and other night creatures would let me know if their songs suddenly stopped that something or someone out of the ordinary was nearby. My HK stuck in my belt at my back and Broken Nose's Hk and rifle were close at hand, but hoped I wouldn't need any of it. One shot and the other hunters would know where we were hiding.

Hard as I tried to stay alert, I dozed off a time or two, losing a half hour here, an hour there, but for the most part, I was awake … jumpy the entire night. I just hoped my adrenalin would keep me sharp when day two of the challenge began.

As light filtered through the brush and into the cave, the last of the night creatures went quiet.

My guest had rolled over during the night to face me. Her breathing was regular. She might still be sleeping, or perhaps awake and planning her next move, I had to count on her not killing me since I saved her life.

I crawled through the brush and examined the area below us. The campfire still smoked, but no motion from the campers snuggled in their sleeping bags.

There was no breeze, yet the grass was waving as though someone was closing in on the campsite. I spotted more movement nearing one of the sleeping bags on the other side of the campfire. Friend or foe … didn't know … didn't care.

My guest moaned and grunted as she moved. I slid back into the cave to check on my roommate. Cheryl turned back to the wall and grunted. As I drew close to check on her she rolled onto her back and said something I didn't understand. She blinked her eyes as though trying to get her bearings. After what she had experienced, I imagined she was trying to figure out what had happened and where she was.

I slid down beside her so she could see my face. Smiling, I stayed just out of reach for my own safety. She grabbed her side, where she kept one of her knives. Even though her eyes were glassy, and she appeared confused, her survival instincts kicked in immediately and she was ready to defend herself as well as control her panic.

Without a knife, muscles stiff and she grimaced in pain, and froze.

I made no sudden moves, but said quietly, "Relax. You're safe. Broken Nose and Neanderthal along with Barbie are dead. At least that's the names I gave them at the compound."

I paused to get her reaction, but there was none.

"I held up my end of the bargain. Had your back, brought you here." I handed her a canteen. "I think you ran on survival instinct while we climbed the mountain and avoided being seen, but you pretty much collapsed and blacked out for the night."

She took small sips of water as she watched me. The intensity in her eyes was frightening. I didn't know if it was fear or a desire to kill. "We are outnumbered and out gunned. It will take the two of us to get out of this situation alive."

She returned the canteen. I offered her a breakfast bar and lit the sterno, I put a pan of water on the burner for coffee.

"This is our second day. We have three or four killers still out there. I spotted some movement and want to keep track of it. Drink some coffee to boost your energy and I'll make us breakfast soon."

I reached out with gentle fingers and checked the damage over her eyes and across her forehead. "Rest for now, you were hit pretty hard yesterday. Your face and temple are bruised. I have pain killers in the medical pack." I said, pointing to the small pile of supplies along the wall. "I hope we can stay hidden today and let the hunters kill each other, then make our way back to the starting point tomorrow."

"After we eat, we can take turns on watch to make sure we aren't compromised. At least one group camped about a mile or so down from us and will continue climbing up the hill and I'm thinking if they find this cave without a lot of trouble, are trapped and eliminated."

Dawn was creeping down our side of the mountain. I slid through the opening. Scanning the area, I refocused my attention on the campsite. Two people charged out of the grass, firing weapons along the ground, ripping sleeping bags to pieces.

I suspected the man was Hulk. Even in his Ghillie, he was tall, big, and walked like he was displaying his muscles on a beach. The woman was much smaller, and her suit was customed to show off her shape.

Cheryl crawled out and lay beside me as the two kicked sleeping bags filled with grass. The camp was empty.

Apparently realizing their mistake, they crouched low and scanned the immediate area.

The crack of a rifle echoed up the hill. A second round followed in less than a second. Hulk fell on the smoldering campfire. The woman pivoted to return fire but flew off her feet after being struck in the shoulder by a high-powered bullet. She was thrown on her back. Pulling off her head gear, Black Widow attempted to use her elbows to help her sit but lacked the strength.

Two, fully camouflaged, figures popped up. One was just a few feet outside the clearing, the other about a hundred yards from the camp. Carrying her rifle in her left hand, Muscle Woman walked up to Black Widow. Kicking her in the chest, flattening her to the ground. She took aim and put a bullet from her pistol in the helpless woman's head.

Beast made his way into the camp and kicked Hulks body out of the fire. The pair gave themselves a high five. They removed head gear. I had the pair identified.

They wasted no time scavenging anything of value from the bodies and what few supplies remained intact. They started a gradual climb hiking parallel to the hill, disappearing in the brush.

"Luck is with us," I said, when they headed west parallel to the hill.

I smiled as I started to crawl back to our hideout. "When they realize no one is off to the side, they will have a steep incline and with a lot of loose rock and boulders to go around or climb over to get back here."

She used the binoculars to track their progress. "They have a steep climb ahead of them just to stay parallel. It would take them at least half the day to get into a higher position before heading back here." She said.

"I call those two 'Beast' and 'Muscle Woman'. I said, the two dead are 'Black Widow' and 'Hulk". 'Barbie,' her former blonde partner, was gutted by Widow just after crossing the yellow tape. Then there is 'Beauty'. She was shot on the first morning and dumped off the trail. I don't know if she is dead or alive."

She nodded. "Two to go, then we can walk down this hill and collect our money".

We re-entered our hide out. I made a quick breakfast of instant oatmeal and coffee. There would be no smell of our meal trapped in our cave and the vines covering the entrance.

We packed everything. "If we bug out, we don't want to forget anything. We have a day and a half before we can make our way to the base." Cheryl commented as she organized her pack and set weapons out ready to grab.

Scanning the area below and off to the side, there was no smoke from a campfire or movement in the grass.

We sat tight, taking one-hour shifts keeping watch and listening for conversation or falling rocks. Night fell, we remained safe in our little hole.

"Those two could double back and set a trap down in the lower jungle." She said handing me the binoculars. "Keep a close look out below us for our two hunters, and don't forget, wounded or dead, watch for the one who is MIA."

I was ready to go in short order and slid out to relieve my partner.

"It would be nice if our two hunters, would turn on each other and we could walk out safe and sound." I said, "And we find our MIA laying halfway down a hill right off the trail."

Shaking her head, Cheryl muttered, "Not much of a chance of that happening."

We ate a quick lunch of protein bars and water. It was mid-day and no sight or sound of Muscle Woman or Beast. "I think we should head down the mountain where there is better cover, find a place to squat for the night." I suggested.

Cheryl agreed, "Good idea, we can search for a spot to ambush them as they make their way to the campground."

We grabbed our equipment and weapons and slid out of the cave and scurried along the outer edge of the mountain. Using my binoculars, I stopped at regular intervals, checking above and below us. I spotted movement up high among the rocks. Our enemy had made better time than I estimated.

We entered the tall grass and it would difficult to see us and impossible to chase at this point.

"Let's get around to the far side of the mountain," Cheryl suggested. "We will be out of their line of sight. We can hot foot it down to the forest."

"Great idea." I agreed, "We can set up a kill zone and eliminate them while they are in the open. They don't seem to be all that interested in hiding their movement."

Cheryl took my field glasses and studied the two as they climbed down from the higher elevation. "They're tired and are sloppy."

She searched the terrain below us. Pointing, she handed me the glasses and pointed to a wide part in the trail with a sharp curve. "I say we take them out. We leave just enough scuffs and trash to get them on the trail and set up the trap on both sides."

I nodded, "The crossfire will keep them from escaping."

Her steel eyes had returned as she studied the layout below. "Let's get down there and discuss how we will handle these two. I would rather be silent and take them by surprise."

We kept track of the progress of our targets. They had made it to the trail - - headed toward us. Their steps were slow, but steady. They would reach the curve in the late afternoon.

"They will probably choose the inside of the curve to camp for the night. Get some rest and start looking for us bright and early." Cheryl said as she studied the layout.

She had extracted one of her knives from the top of her boots. "We do them before they get off the trail."

Stroking the blade like a lover, she talked quietly to herself. "It would be easy to sneak up and simply cut their throats." Leaning her head back, she ran the flat part of the blade across her throat. "The blade is razor sharp and can probably take the head right off the body."

Her eyes seemed to sparkle when she placed the point of the knife at the back of my neck. "A lot more fun to throw and put the blade in the back of the spine."

She moved the blade away from my neck and commented, "The body continues to live for a bit, but eventually they fall." Her devious grin and demonstration showed me she was the voice of experience. Either is quick and quiet. After that, whoever is closer to the next target deals with them."

Standing on the side of the trail, her body was stiff as a board … it was taunt like a coiled spring ready to lash out. Her eyes became pin pricks as they moved from side to side. I knew she was visualizing the kills … just as I had done when in the Seals.

I couldn't stop staring at her. I knew this was her assassin side, and I was happy that she didn't have a target on my back.

"At least it won't have to be quiet for the second person." She sounded disappointed.

As we continued down the trail, I kept my eye out for 'Beauty". I couldn't remember where her body had been dumped. I would feel better if she were already dead and not waiting for the last survivor to be moseying down the trail and collecting a bullet instead of the prize money.

We crept our way through the weeds and vines. The downward direction wasn't the problem, but as our feet slid on the vines and underbrush, moving with stealth was challenging. I prayed our killer competition were out of range, unable to hear our thrashing through the bushes. I hoped we could spot them, adjust our ambush plan, and kill them before they realized we were waiting.

It took us until early afternoon before we arrived at our ambush location.

"Based on their progress, they should pass by our position in an hour or so." Cheryl said. "Let's do this quietly, if this 'Beauty" is alive, no need using fire-arms to tell her where we are.

Once we arrived, I hid about fifteen feet in the tall weeds on the outside of the bend. I had my bow ready to kill the lead person. My Glock was holstered at my side in case I missed with the arrow.

Cheryl, her knife ready to draw blood, stepped into the weeds on the steep inside curve. I lost her as soon as she knelt in the brush.

She had to be close to the worn path. "I'm going to come up behind one of them and slit their throat." She had said earlier.

I remained fifteen feet or so away from my target. I could kneel or stand and put an arrow through the person before they realized I was there.

I heard heavy grunting and complaining long before they came into view.

"Damn, I need a break, we can't go in until tomorrow and we still got the two losers to put down." Muscle woman whined. "My legs are cramping, and I need a break.

"I thought you were physically fit. What did you do, juice up your muscles, and now a real workout tears you down?" Beast's growled back at her.

She gave him the finger. "Those two are probably hiding out somewhere. They wouldn't head towards the finish line until tomorrow. We can take a break, find a spot to rest for now. Later we climb a couple of trees and take them out as they slink by."

"Stop if you want, but I'm moving on. Once I lose sight of you, it's is open season, unless you want to stop, rest and allow me to enjoy your body." He laughed.

"That's Erick's pleasure, not yours. God, why didn't I stay in the meadow instead of joining you in this hunt? It's not like you are getting into my pants." She spit in anger.

"Having had to take care of you the past couple days, I have earned that pleasure," He said. "And I don't care if I have you or here, or back in the compound and possible a third time when we reach civilization. You will pleasure me and keep quiet. If you talk, Erick is a dead meat. He may be my good friend and work out partner, but I'll put a bullet in him before he realizes he is a dead man."

Beast laughed at his own joke. "Of course, I could wound him and let him watch."

Realizing what he just said, he added, "and just

remember, we became a team when we lost our partners, so don't get any ideas of getting rid of me and sharing the money with him."

They rounded the bend. The path narrowed, Muscle Woman dropped back a few steps.

Cheryl let her get six steps past her before she crept onto the trail and kept pace behind them, unnoticed.

'Beast' continued sharing what he would do to his partner. "Hell, for all I care, I could possess every inch of you in a cabin while we wait for our ride out of here. Erick doesn't have to know."

"Oh, don't worry, Erick is known as the 'Glimmer Man' you won't see him coming. After I tell him you raped me, he will make sure you have a long painful death." She touted, "Give that some thought and keep your fantasies to yourself."

Her snarky response was answered by an angry snort. She stopped walking, putting herself out of reach if he decided to back hand her.

It was the snort that allowed Cheryl to attack. She took three long steps and drove her knife's blade deep into the back of Muscle Woman's neck - - she separated the bones in her neck and pushed point of the blade through the throat. With both hands, she twisted the blade which destroyed her airway and severed the spinal column.

She caught the body and lowered it quietly to the ground.

Arrow notched and ready. As Beast turned to see what the noise was behind him, I stood and fired into the side of Beast's chest, exploding a lung, and possibly injuring a few other organs, including his heart.

His expression registered surprise then confusion as he stared at the shaft protruding from his body. His mouth moved soundlessly as he dropped to his knees. He fell to the side.

"Well done, Harold. How does your first kill feel?" Cheryl asked.

I shrugged my shoulders, "It wasn't my first. I killed to save you. I'm not sick, elated or feeling sorry for him. Given another two seconds or so, he would have put a bullet in my head. I can deal with it."

She shrugged. "Well, I hope you don't have too many nightmares after this experience. Killing someone tends to stay with you, until you make a habit of it."

I made my way up to the trail and collected my arrow. I started walking and Cheryl joined me.

We left the bodies where they lay. As far as I was concerned, they could rot, or the hired help could go out and collect them. We made our way toward the compound.

"I'm still not sure about Beauty being alive or dead." I said, "I think it would be wise if we staggered ourselves on the path and stay as quiet as possible.

Cheryl gave me a thumbs up.

We walked for over an hour, staying at opposite edges of the path and several feet apart. My head was on a swivel looking high and low for Beauty.

I spotted her halfway up a tree, straddling a limb. I stopped and signaled Cheryl and pointed towards our opponent's position. Beauty's head was turning in our direction as she scanned the area.

We hugged the ground—not even moving enough to breath.

"I'll move in close to get a shot, you take the other side of the trail and back me up." She said in a quiet voice. "I will give us ten minutes to get into position."

Beauty scanned away from us with small head turns. She was using an excellent technique to cover the trail and surrounding brush. "We should be safe as long as she is looking in the other direction." I commented.

With a thumbs up, she rolled down into the grass and headed for the trees. Following her lead, I duck crawled into the grass.

Keeping one eye on the tree, I moved deeper into the brush as Beauty looked in the opposite direction. I found a spot, out of range, that allowed me observe and keep track of her.

I focused my field glasses on the limb, I had a clear view of the woman.

She had made a major mistake waiting for our return. the white bandage on her across her shoulder gave me a clear target. She forgot to cover white tape with brush or dirt. I now had the perfect angle to take her out. If Cheryl couldn't see the bandage, her camo outfit would position her on the tree. It was full of dead vegetation and not the leaves from the tree. This would give her a clear shot. We both had her dead to rights.

I changed my position and would use my bow to knock her out of the tree. I had a straight shot, but needed to get across the trail to have the range and accuracy to match my ability to hit her.

I dropped back down to the ground when her head turned in my direction once more. Looking through her binoculars, her head swiveled and lifted, as though searching the higher parts of the mountain as well as the valley.

Checking my watch, there were two minutes before our attack. I notched my arrow. Cheryl had her rifle and could shoot from a greater distance.

Beauty looked away from me. I got up and shot across the path and slid down the incline. I had thirty seconds to set up my shot.

As I closed in on her, I heard her talking to herself. "Where are those two half-wits? Bet there out there playing touchy feely instead of looking for those two singles. If I see them, I'll kill all four of them and get all the money for myself."

I knew the ten minutes were up as two shots rang out at Beauty. She jerked back against the tree and turned her weapon in the direction of the shooter. I stood and launched my arrow in her lower abdomen.

Beauty fell from the tree.

Cheryl ran toward the woman.

"She's breathing, but I don't think we are in any danger." I said checking her pulse.

Cheryl brought the sharp edge of her knife to Beauty's neck and sliced to the bone. "First rule of gladiators ... a wounded enemy can still kill you." She said smiling. "You do realize, the game is over."

We held hands and had some small conversation as we made our way down to the compound. I couldn't suppress the cocky smile ... I survived. All our competitors had been vanquished. I can live with half the prize, I told myself.

Cheryl's hand felt good in mine. I had to admit I hoped we had a future together. After all we had been through, I felt a bond between us.

We didn't want to enter the compound until the official start of the next day. We relaxed by the tape indicating the beginning of the encampment and spoke in quiet tones, as we hid in the weeds. Sometime during the night, Cheryl, despite the dirt, grime, and blood, began removed her clothing and mine.

When she finished with me, I whispered, "I hope this is the beginning of a long and happy relationship."

She gave a grunt but said nothing as she rolled over and went to sleep.

Once the sun rose above the mountains and began lighting the compound, we ducked under the yellow tape and made our way into camp.

Cheryl had not spoken since we woke and dressed. She wouldn't acknowledge any talk of plans for the future. I shook my head and told myself to be satisfied with last night and let it go.

Our feet crunched in the dirt and gravel as we entered the

encampment. She silently dropped back a few steps. She was keeping pace but not the stride. I realized I couldn't hear her walking behind me. At that moment, my mind flashed … Oh shit!

I reached up with my left hand and pulled out my survival knife from my waist band and held it down the side of my leg.

I couldn't forget how she stabbed 'Muscle Woman" from behind and sliced 'Beauty's throat without making a sound or having a second thought. I focused on her footsteps hoping for a sound, any sound that would tell me I was wrong.

Ringer stepped out of his hut and stretched. He watched us approach and smiled. At that instant, I 'stumbled', my head dropping down out of the line of attack. Stepping back, I plunged my 'knife' straight toward any attacker, hoping to find nothing but air. I felt resistance, as the metal impaled itself into something soft. I turned and saw the look of surprise on her face as the knife buried itself up through her diaphragm and into her left lung.

Cheryl stood, her razored blade in hand, ready to plunge it into the back of my neck. I held the pummel of my weapon with both hands and pushed up at an angle destroying any vital organs in its path.

She didn't scream as she dropped to her knees. With a twist, I pulled out my composite blade. Her insides flowed to the ground like a fountain in summer.

"Why? Why?" I asked her, "We made it, we could collect the money and live new lives, why try to kill me?"

Her mouth moved but only blood fell from her lips. Ringer walked up to us. He used his boot to kick her in the chest. She fell backward, eyes glazing in death.

"She knew that only one of you could survive. You two weren't a designated team."

I looked at him with no emotion. "You mean she knew she had to kill me before we even began the game or teamed up?"

He nodded. "Yes, and to be honest, I didn't figure either of you would survive. You can never be sure how the Fates decide what goes on in these challenges."

He started walking toward the kitchen. "Come, get some breakfast, I'll call the plane and get you the money. Have a nice flight back to the real world."

Hours later, the first of my two planes touched down. I carried two bags and a backpack. The backpack had the money, the other two my clothing and weapons.

Funny though, I returned to my job, invested, and divested the money and kept the entire adventure a secret. When asked, I simply said I attended a survival school that lasted several days, plus travel. It was a grueling experience and I was happy to be home.

"Yes, I was injured, nothing serious," I explained, "but that is part of the training. Better to be wounded and remember than to be dead for not being aware of anything."

A year later, I joined the ranks of the unemployed and started living off my investment interest.

I sometimes think of Cheryl and how I wish things could have turned out in a different way, split the money, meet up and live happily after. But that's not the way things go sometimes. Plus…I didn't have to share.

ABOUT THE AUTHOR

Born in East St. Louis, John spent a major portion of his youth in Illinois. He began reading at an early age and soon discovered a love for science fiction and horror.

He devoured book after book about vampires, shifters, and dragons.

John holds a degree in journalism from the University of Memphis (formerly Memphis State University).

His military career included twelve years in Public Affairs in the United States Airforce. It was his military experience that honed his writing skills as he won several awards.

After retiring from the Air Force, he bought a Harley and volunteered with politically active motorcycle organizations. He wrote stories promoting motorcycling, events, and safety. These articles were published throughout the state of California. He was also a contributor to multiple international motorcycle magazines.

John currently lives in Highland, Illinois with his dog "Hurricane Ollie".

John invites our comments and thought his books. You can email John at www. writerphotographer1946@gmail.com AND post a review on Amazon.

John is available to speak at conventions and seminars. You can contact him at www. writerphotographer1946@gmail.com

To find out where John is appearing visit his website at www.johnwsmithauthor.com

SHORT STORIES

NIGHTMARES OF A MAD MAN

A collection of short stories that travel through the dark side of the mind. Written in the vein of Tales from the Dark Side, Tales from the Crypt, and Twilight Zone, there are twists and turns through the book. The stories travel from light (easy to read to smaller children), to very dark for adult readers.

Little Miss Moffett … meets a different kind of spider in this story.

The Caress … A young woman falls in love with an art collector. Will she pose for him?

Autumn Leaves … What if the leaves aren't ready to become mulch?

These stories allow you to select what story would cause a mad man, living in a room with padded walls, suddenly sit up, screaming from a dream. You get to choose.

Amazon https://amzn.to/34lyYvU

DARK DREAMS

John's second book of short stories can be considered dark fiction and contains a variety of creatures, great and small. Some appear cuddly … but wait, there's more. There are people you will meet may be paranoid, but that doesn't mean the government isn't out to get them.

A Father gives his daughter an antique doll who has some very special

qualities, and not all are pleasant.

Here you will find modern day computers … Artificial Intelligence, some would argue … but are they here to serve mankind?

Travel down the rabbit hole through seventeen adventures. Enjoy the twists and turns in the stories. Remember as you read …

THERE ARE NO HAPPY ENDINGS IN DARK DREAMS.

Amazon. https://amzn.to/2FKInmh

NOVELS

TAINTED BLOOD

A legendary castle, located in Eastern Europe, built into an unknown mountainside. It houses the Princess Selene of the Woodlands. It is said she rules over the dark creatures of the night and each decade, she holds an All Hallows Eve Ball, inviting selected powerful men to the event. The winner has their lives changed forever.

The men never return home and the rumors abound that Selene is a witch or something worse. Others believe she grants riches and sends the men to the new worlds to grow rich and powerful, in her name.

The story begins some 700 years prior to today. Sir William of the Highlands receives an invitation and attends the Ball. He never returns.

The story jumps to present days. William's family, gypsies who have lived under the veil of Selene, train the first-born descendant male to go into the world and to kill William, end the curse, and avenge the family name.

A story of Good vs. Evil. Sometimes Evil wins, Sometimes Good wins, but is there ever a happy ending.

Amazon. https://amzn.to/3aTQOHt

NOVELETTE

DEATH'S RETRIBUTION

Sylvia Devlin has buried six husbands. Some call her unlucky at love, others call her a black widow. After the funeral of her most recent husband, an apparition appears in the mist and talks to Sylvia. Each visit to the grave, he appears and tells of her past, present, and future.

When He informs her that she is not the owner of the foundry her husband built, she is also told that she will house the new owner during his visit. When he arrives, she decides she can become excessively wealthy if he becomes her next conquest.

Things do not turn out as she had planned. What goes around comes around because Karma is a bitch.

Amazon Paper Back. https://amzn.to/2CVAYQe

Kindle https://amzn.to/2EctwAW

HEART OF A DRAGON

A Novelette about an attorney named Sherman Davis. Sherman is a successful attorney with a trophy wife. She is a tyrant. Spends his money on needless things for herself, runs in a variety of circles that include country clubs, charity organizations, and young lovers.

One evening Lenora is charging through the mall, Sherman in tow when he hears a voice coming from the window of a toy story. A green dragon hand puppet sends out a greeting. Sherman stops and talks with the creature, and much to his wife's anger, purchases the puppet.

Puff … As named by Sherman. The two become best friends. Puff teaches him to stand up for himself.

The wife vows vengeance but is in for a surprise.

Amazon Paper Back https://amzn.to/3lan6mn

Kindle. https://amzn.to/2Ys3xfM

ANTHOLOGY

John produced and coordinated the production of A Dark and Stormy Night, an anthology. The work had two challenges for the writers. First the dark and stormy night and second a total of 1,500 words per story.

A DARK AND STORMY NIGHT, AN ANTHOLOGY

Stories written by seventeen different writers. There are two from California, one from Kentucky and the remainder reside in Southern Illinois.

Explore how people visualize a dark and stormy night. What do they fear? Weather, Monsters, People or is it modern day life that hides in the dark corners of their minds.

Explore the storms and choose which one forces you to turn all the lights on at night.

John has been included in a variety of Anthologies. He doesn't make a habit of contributing as it reminds him of deadlines as an Air Force Journalist. He prefers to work on his material as he prefers to work on several project at a time. These are the three most recent since his retirement.

Amazon. https://amzn.to/3lfixr8

WORDS TO READ

John has several stories in the book.

This book is currently out of print, however you can order a copy through Charles Schwend, the writer who produced the book. Additional information can be found the the link above.

Order books directly: Chuck Schwend's email is schwendcharles@yahoo.com

https://amzn.to/2ExOQAk

THE WRITE STUFF

This anthology created by the Carlinville Writers Guild has a variety of stories from the members of the group, including John. All proceeds are used to support the guild.

Amazon https://amzn.to/3ldfcZB

PRETTY GOOD STUFF

This anthology created by the Carlinville Writers Guild has a variety of stories from member of the group, including John. All proceeds are used to support the group.

Amazon. https://amzn.to/3aRfK2A

E-SHORT STORIES

John has published a total of three e-short stories. Two can be found on Kindle as well as several other venues. The Third story (*Spirit Dagger*) has been pulled as he is turning this story into a novel and will be available in 2021.

COLONIAL SCUM

It is a time of peace, however there is a rebel faction rising within the kingdom. It is rumored that the leader of the group will be at a meeting and the location is passed down to the royal guard.

An officer crashes into the meeting and kills the person he thought was the leader … it was his beloved. He now seeks revenge not only on the "Colonial Scum" but also on the leader.

Amazon. https://amzn.to/32bDCcY

HUNGRY THINGS

Have you ever had a dream so real you woke up knowing the event happened and you were there? This short story is about a group of adventurers who when they sleep travel to a new dimension. They leave the comforts of the 21st century to travel to a medieval time on a different world.

They are "sell swords", but they defend the poor and helpless. They hear of something that destroys villages and all living life is gone. They go in search of the things called "The Widows". They discover a terrible creature that can destroy this world.

The Travelers also discover a group of women in their own world … a tough motorcycle gang known as the Black Widows. Are the two connected, can they defeat an enemy in two worlds?

This book has lots of adventure and fighting of monsters in two dimensions.

Amazon. https://amzn.to/2Yu4Hax

www.ingramcontent.com/pod-product-compliance
Lightning Source LLC
Chambersburg PA
CBHW071927220626
47052CB00002B/486